CELEBRITY

SIENNA SNOW

ISBN - 978-1-948756-01-3 (Print)

POLITICS OF LOVE

CELEBRITY

BOOK 1

Sienna Snow

ACKNOWLEDGMENTS

I wanted to give a heartfelt thank you to JoDeen Anderson. You have kept me sane so many times when I've gotten overwhelmed and had no clue what I was doing. You are a true gem, and I am so glad you are my friend and wrangler.

As always, to my sweet husband, who puts up with all my craziness and still loves me. Thank you for keeping our family on track when I'm in my writing cave and for drawing me a hot bath when I'm on the verge of collapse.

CHAPTER ONE

"Counselor. Please approach the bench."

I held in an internal groan as I stood and moved around the defendant's table. The judge was determined to make my life hell in the courtroom.

My day had started off with a mix of determination and excitement. I'd deal with the standard back-and-forth of my current case and then planned to spend the evening decompressing.

However, everything had changed when I'd arrived at the courthouse. A new judge had been assigned to my case because of a family emergency, and now I was stuck dealing with the backlash of a judge that didn't particularly care for me. It was as if my mere presence annoyed the crap out of Judge McGregor, and for the life of me, I couldn't figure out why.

Our only interaction had been at a social event where

she'd arrived as my ex-lover's date. If anyone should have been annoyed, it was me.

I shook the thought from my head and focused on Judge McGregor. I couldn't wait until this afternoon. In less than one hour, I'd no longer be lead on this case, and I could start planning the next phase of my career.

"I don't have all day, Counselor. You may enjoy the sensationalism of this case, but I don't."

"Yes, Your Honor," I responded and approached the judge.

If she only knew the truth of how I felt about my newfound celebrity. I liked life behind the scenes and in the background, or at least I had until Clint Bassett became my client four months ago.

I glanced at him to give him an unsaid order to behave. He responded with a wink and air kisses, and then followed it up by popping open the collar of his shirt.

I clenched my jaw and took a deep breath.

His bright green eyes danced with mischief, and the groupies behind him fawned over every one of his movements.

Clint used his public platform to project an asshole persona. People either loved him or hated him.

He enjoyed the media attention. Both good and bad. Hell, his attitude was the reason half of the world thought he deserved the grief he was getting. Clint was a shock jock and proud of it. Ruffling feathers was his job. He had a knack for getting politicians and celebrities irritated and spilling their secrets, many times without meaning to.

No matter what his public image, he didn't deserve this lawsuit. Judge McGregor knew it, the media knew it, and even the person who was suing him knew it.

This case had dragged on for over four months, and I was tired. I'd sacrificed my personal life and my privacy for Clint, leaving anyone close to me a target for scrutiny.

No matter where I went, I was followed, and finding out who I was dating was a mission Clint's fans were determined to learn. Something that had caused me more pain than I wished to think about.

Even though this case had become the bane of my existence, I planned to use it to my benefit.

"Ms. Kumar, these disruptions will no longer be tolerated. We haven't officially started today's session, and we've had three outbursts because of your client. I'm tempted to clear the room."

Judge McGregor said my name with disgust, as if the words left a foul taste in her mouth. What was her problem?

I couldn't wait to wash my hands of this mess.

The basis of the whole lawsuit was due to hurt feelings and vengeance, not fact. However, if one had an unending bank account and limitless time, the top attorneys in the country would happily take your case. And my client's ex-wife, Kimberly Bassett, had both in ample supply.

Yes, I was a celebrity attorney, and I'd had my fair share of media coverage, but usually my clients wanted their names kept out of the press. They rarely catered to it.

"With all due respect, Your Honor. Mr. Travis, Ms.

Bassett's counsel, is the one who requested this hearing be open to the public. It isn't my client's fault so many have come out in support of him, even on a non-court day."

At that moment, a bunch of shouts and cheers erupted.

Then someone said, "You tell her, Hot Stuff. Don't let this new judge give you shit. She probably hasn't had her oil changed in years with that sour face of hers."

I cringed, closing my eyes for a brief second. Insulting the judge was not going to help me, and neither was calling me sexist names.

Clint had given me the nickname on his radio show, and since that day, all his millions of fans referred to me as "Hot Stuff."

He'd thrown me into the media spotlight, not only for my skills but my looks. This was not how I'd planned to make a name for myself when I'd graduated law school at the top of my class.

I had never wanted this case in the first place, but my law partner, Tara Zain, was handling a high-profile murder trial that had left me as the only viable option.

The things my client said disgusted me on most days. His only redeeming factor was that he kept a distinct line between his personal and public lives. He wasn't a jerk in real life. He was a nice guy who loved his kids and, until recently, his ex-wife.

"I'm up here, Counselor." Judge McGregor glared down at me.

One day I was going to find out why this woman hated me.

I missed Judge Trammel. She loved to hand me my ass, but she was fair and took no one's bullshit. It wasn't her fault that her husband had a heart attack and she'd had to leave the case.

"Your client's celebrity status is the reason this case has gone on as long as it has. From what Judge Trammel conveyed, you've become a celebrity yourself."

I ignored the last part of her statement and responded to the first. "I disagree, Your Honor. The length of this meaningless case is due to Ms. Bassett's need to continue her five minutes of fame after her divorce for cheating on her husband."

Damn, I shouldn't have added the last part.

"How dare you? You're just another one of his tramps. I'll ruin you. If it's the last thing I do. I'll ruin you!"

Judge McGregor rapped her gavel. "Counselor, get Ms. Bassett under control, or I'll remove her from the courtroom. Threatening opposing counsel is a chargeable offense."

The woman needed to learn new insults. She'd called me tramp and whore so many times that I'd lost count.

It didn't matter much longer anyway. I wouldn't be on the case after today. I was going to transition my client to Karina Taylor, one of the junior attorneys in my law firm. She was foaming at the mouth to defend this case. She wanted to make her mark in the world and prove she was qualified to become a partner.

From the look on Karina's face as she sat next to Clint, I could tell she was shocked by how this non-session had started. I hadn't been able to get a real word in, and I wasn't even sure if Judge McGregor was aware I no longer represented Clint.

"I didn't threaten that whore," Kimberly countered.

I felt the distinct urge to walk up to her and smack her.

The way things were looking, even with Judge Trammel's approval for attorney change, I was never going to be able to leave this courthouse.

It took another ten minutes to get Kimberly and the media under control.

I could see a vein pulsing on the side of Judge McGregor's face.

Celebrity divorce scandals weren't her usual type of proceeding. She spent most of her days dealing with murder trials and felony litigations.

She glanced between the opposing attorney and me. "I'd like to see both parties in my office. We will discuss this case without distractions so that I am brought up to speed with the numerous changes Judge Trammel approved before she stepped down."

She rapped her gavel, then released an exasperated sigh as she stood and spoke again. "Once this is over, Ms. Kumar, I hope I never have to encounter you in a courtroom again. Your celebrity clients could encourage the most pious person to drink."

Ten minutes later, the courtroom was cleared, and our clients and their respective entourages were the only ones left.

Opposing counsel Nathan Travis and I made our way

to the hallway leading to Judge McGregor's private office. I glanced over my shoulder toward Clint, who had a pained expression as he gazed at Kimberly.

Poor man—he still loved her.

Then I took a peek at Kimberly, and she had a similar yearning in her eyes. She was trying to ignore Clint, but every so often she'd glance his way, and her lip would tremble.

They had been happily married for twenty years before one stupid, yet enormous, mistake destroyed it all.

Turning back to follow Nathan down the corridor, I shook my head.

"If they end up back together, I'm going to be so pissed that I wasted four months of my life on this case," I muttered to myself.

"You and me both," I thought I heard a distinct Louisiana accent mumble.

I paused, inhaled deep, and looked to my side. Devin Camden, the one man who starred in every one of my fantasies, sat on a bench, reading a newspaper. He oozed Southern charm without uttering a word, but then when he spoke, any woman with a pulse had to keep her panties from melting.

His sky-blue gaze bored into mine, making my pulse accelerate and reminding me of things best left forgotten.

Why did I have to run into him today?

We had too much history, and our careers ran on separate paths.

He was the type of man I'd always dreamed of being

with: strong, confident, self-assured, with an edge that screamed rebel bad boy.

He came from a long line of conservative Louisiana senators. Politics was in his blood. However, to his family's dismay, he'd chosen a different route for his life. He'd moved to a new state, pursuing a law career outside of the political spotlight, and desired a simple existence.

With his looks and manner, he made the sexy prime minister of Canada look like a wimpy old geezer. And below his gorgeous face was a body chiseled to perfection and ideal for the covers of magazines.

Shit, I had to stop thinking about him like that. He was a federal magistrate judge whose career came before a relationship with a celebrity attorney.

There was a slight smirk on his too-good-looking-for-his-own-good face. God, he was such a cocky bastard. He knew how he affected me.

He'd have to remain in the world of make-believe and lost possibilities.

Nathan touched my arm, returning my attention to the task at hand. I knocked on the office door and entered when summoned. We'd arrived as the judge moved to her desk.

"Have a seat. This shouldn't take long without either of your clients present."

Nathan and I took our spots on the other side of the large oak monstrosity.

I could almost envision Judge Camden being the one before us, taking off his robe, hanging it on a hook near him. I pictured his muscled arms bunching and bulging under the fitted white button-down shirts he favored. The thought made me nearly swallow my tongue.

What I wouldn't give to lick every inch of that body again.

A throat cleared, making me refocus on Judge McGregor.

What the hell was I doing?

My hormones were going haywire. It had been too long since I'd gotten laid. The last thing I needed was to have Judge McGregor hate me even more because I wasn't paying attention.

"Counselors, we didn't even get to start today's discussion without chaos ensuing. Do I need to make it clear that you have to keep your clients under control?"

Before I could respond, a knock sounded on the door, and Devin Camden's head peeked inside.

Of course, the man I was envisioning licking would be the one to interrupt the meeting.

"Oh, excuse me." His gaze held mine as he spoke to Judge McGregor. "I didn't realize you were meeting with the counselors. I'll come back later."

"No, Devin. Don't worry about it. We will finish in a moment. Just take a seat over there." Judge McGregor gestured to a set of couches in the back of the room.

"Samina. Nathan," he greeted Nathan and me.

"Judge Camden," I responded and inclined my head.

"Devin."

"Excuse me?" I said, not sure why he'd said his name.

"Out there, I'm Judge Camden. Out of the public eye, I'm Devin."

No way in hell was I calling him by his first name right now, no matter our history. I peeked at Nathan, who shrugged his shoulders. Nathan and the judge played golf together, and he never called him by his first name when in work mode. Our relationship was frosty at best to justify any familiarity.

This was a test. It had to be.

"Judge Camden, it's good to see you, as always." Nathan broke the standoff between Judge Camden and me.

"I doubt you'll be saying that tomorrow after eighteen holes," he answered Nathan but held my gaze as he sat down and pulled out his phone.

"Ms. Kumar, you may continue." Judge McGregor checked her watch as if I was wasting her time.

I took a deep breath and spoke. "My client has been on his best behavior, Your Honor. He was willing to settle this in private, but Ms. Bassett wanted it aired in a courtroom as well as in the court of public opinion."

"Do you have anything to counter, Mr. Travis?"

Nathan shook his head. "I do what my client wants, and she wants to make her ex-husband suffer. I would rather be spending my weekends with my wife and kids."

"I take it you aren't enjoying the notoriety of this case?" Judge McGregor watched me, but asked Nathan the question.

"Let's say my family prefers a quieter existence."

"What about you, Ms. Kumar?"

"I'm not following, Your Honor."

"You've become a celebrity in your own right. You're on the cover of at least four magazines and half the people filling the courtroom were there for you. What does your family have to say about this?"

She looked behind me toward Judge Camden, telling me she was aware of my past with him.

Shit, how many people knew about us?

"It's complicated things."

If she only had a small inclination of the true depths of how difficult my life had become.

"How so?" Judge Camden asked from behind us, surprising not only me and Nathan but Judge McGregor too.

I turned, glaring at him for a brief second before I returned my gaze to Judge McGregor.

"My private life is just that, private. I do not like it invaded. That is the reason I sent my special request to Judge Trammel last week. One that she approved before your assignment to preside over the case."

A frown appeared on her face. "What request?"

She searched through the stack of papers on her desk.

"As of this afternoon, Karina Taylor will take over Mr. Bassett's litigation."

"What?" both Nathan and Judge Camden said in unison.

"Sam, you aren't serious." Nathan gave me a pleading

look. "Kim's going to lose her mind when she finds out someone even younger than you will defend Clint."

"What does Karina's age have to do with anything?"

"You don't know?" Nathan stared at me like I was clueless.

Was I missing something? I glanced at Judge McGregor, who shrugged her shoulders. "Mr. Travis, both Ms. Kumar and I are confused by your statement. Care to enlighten us?"

Nathan's face reddened with embarrassment, and he pulled at his collar. He turned to me and spoke. "Sam, you're, umm...you know, you. And it's... How do I put this without being sexist and completely out of line? Never mind, I'm keeping my mouth shut."

"Nathan, I'm not following this train of thought either." I furrowed my brow.

"Let me clarify for you, Samina," Judge Camden said from behind me. "What Nathan is attempting to say is that you are a very attractive person who happens to make Ms. Bassett very jealous. And changing to another attorney who is equally attractive but younger will not bode well for Mr. Travis."

When was being thirty considered old? Besides, Karina was only a year younger.

"Honestly, that isn't my problem."

I tried to have sympathy for Nathan, but his life wasn't the one on perpetual hold. I couldn't step outside my home without a camera pointed in my direction. If I was going to be a celebrity, I'd rather it be on my terms and not as part of a media spectacle.

Because of this case, my life was in complete shambles. The man I'd thought I'd spend the rest of my life with couldn't look at me without getting angry, and I was left to live in fantasies. My friends hated going anywhere in public with me, not to mention there was no way in hell I could spend a night out on the town without causing more problems for myself.

"Ms. Kumar, I have to say, I respect your decision," Judge McGregor said. "I was in your shoes before I took my current position. It isn't one I wish to revisit. I have to say, I'm impressed how you've maintained a solid reputation, considering your poor choice in clients."

Okay, was that a compliment? Maybe she didn't hate me after all.

"Thank you." I checked my watch. "Your Honor, I'd like to return to my client before anything unexpected happens."

It wouldn't surprise me if Clint had arranged a wrestling match between his and his ex-wife's supporters.

"I agree. We don't need any more spectacles. I'll announce the changes to the case. Congratulations, Ms. Kumar. You are no longer representing Clint Bassett. Good day, Ms. Kumar. Mr. Travis."

CHAPTER TWO

S ix hours after leaving the courthouse, I opened the door to my beautiful house and sighed. Thank God the hired security had my place protected like Fort Knox. The last thing I needed was another incident with an overzealous reporter—one break-in to capture the perfect picture was more than enough for this lifetime.

The paparazzi camped out along the front of my property, waiting for any sighting of me, and all I wanted was a large glass of wine and a sexy-as-sin man in my life. Preferably, someone like Devin Camden but without the career ramifications.

The wine I had in hundreds of bottles, the man was another matter.

After the roller coaster of a day I'd had, I might just pass out from exhaustion following a scalding shower and forgo the alcohol.

True to form, Clint and Kimberly had continued their

love/hate behavior with long, sad looks and a complete meltdown from Kimberly when Nathan informed her that Karina was now lead for Clint. Nathan could have at least waited until Karina and I had exited the courtroom before sharing the good news.

On the positive side, I was officially on vacation for the next month and a half. Sometimes it was good to be the boss. I still had briefs to review, documents to draft, and planning to conduct, but those were things I could do for the most part from my kitchen island, in my PJs, with a cup of coffee. Besides, I'd more than earned this break by putting in nonstop hundred-hour weeks for over four months.

I planned to savor every moment of this stay-cation. The second it ended, I'd begin a new chapter of my life that would require more energy than I'd expended on the Bassett case. Too bad these new steps would be as a single woman.

I dropped my purse and keys on the front table and then took in the view from the floor-to-ceiling windows overlooking the Sound.

I finally had a home of my own. I'd moved out of the cramped condo in downtown Seattle a week before the trial started and into a place where I could see myself living the rest of my days.

The house was two years of blood, sweat, and tears. Who knew building a house on the Puget Sound would take so long? In the end, it was worth it.

Nine thousand square feet of water views, a chef's

kitchen, and a backyard that rivaled the landscape at a five-star resort. This was my dream home, built because of the success that came after years filled with long hours, little sleep, and limitless drive. And not a dime of it came from my father or my trust fund, something I'm sure annoyed my father to no end.

However, moving in had been bittersweet. I'd hoped it would have been with the man of my dreams, my partner, my husband, the father of my future children, but life had other plans.

I had no one to blame but myself.

I walked through the house to the doors leading to the back patio, and then to the half wall overlooking the beach below the cliffs.

Gripping the iron railing, I closed my eyes and envisioned piercing blue ones gazing at me with love and laughter. Something I hadn't experienced in so long—over eighteen months, to be exact.

This man would see past the public persona to the woman underneath and still love me. He would accept my need for success as much as I did his. He wouldn't hide what we were to each other, but be proud of it.

What I wanted could all be a dream, but I refused to give up hope. I'd thought I'd had it once, and it could happen again.

Maybe.

At that moment, I felt a presence behind me. The scent of soap and crisp cologne hit my senses.

Dammit, what did he want? How many times were we going to rehash the same fight, the same pain?

He couldn't get over what my life had become and would continue to be, and I was tired of trying to make him understand. It wasn't as if I'd chosen the fame or the notoriety.

His career couldn't be the only thing that mattered.

"Are you still mad at me?" I asked without turning.

I gripped the railing tight and stared out at the waves rippling behind a passing boat.

"No."

"If you're here for another act to our unending fight, I just don't have the energy or the time for it today." I couldn't hide the tremble in my voice.

Dammit, Samina. You're not supposed to let him see how much it hurts.

His presence was throwing me as it was, and an argument was only going to cause me to say something I'd regret later.

"No, that's not why I wanted to see you."

"Then why are you here? Aren't you afraid one of the paps will photograph you? You might end up on the cover of a tabloid magazine if you're not careful."

He stepped closer to me, making me stiffen. I could almost feel his body heat behind me.

"No. I took the private walkway from the neighbor's property. I'm the one who hired your security, so they let me pass."

"The closest neighbor is half a mile away."

"Was that a question?"

Irritation prickled my temper, and I inhaled deep to stay calm. "I guess you are here to pick a fight, and as I said moments ago, I'm not in the mood. You can leave the way you came."

I continued to gaze at the deep blue depths flowing in front of me. Maybe if I ignored him, he'd go away. Combined with everything that had happened in court today and the constant reminders of my failed relationship, there wasn't any energy left to deal with my ex.

I was barely coping as it was.

"I'm here for only one purpose."

"And what is that?" I turned to face him, and my heart skipped a beat as I took in the man standing before me.

He was breathtaking. A light sheen of sweat from his hike covered his dark brows. He'd thrown his suit jacket over his shoulder and his shirtsleeves were rolled up. His normally impeccable sandy-brown hair was windblown, giving me an urge to run my fingers through it as I'd done countless times.

"I'm here for you. It's been weeks since I touched you. I miss you. I need you."

He stepped forward, making me press against the railing.

"Go away. What happened at the courthouse today doesn't change anything."

His face grew angry. "All I wanted. All I ever wanted was for you to pick me first. To make me the priority and not the media darling you've become. You did that today."

"No." I shook my head. "I picked you first, years ago. You never saw it. You were so wrapped up in making partner and then the federal magistrate appointment to notice. I told my father to go fuck himself when he made me choose between my inheritance and you. I haven't spoken to him in over five years. Do you have any idea what it's like not to have your mother at your wedding? I picked you, but you never saw it.

"When I made my career a priority, you couldn't take it. I never wanted to hide our relationship, you did. What happened today was for me. I'm making myself a priority for the first time in my life."

He moved in front of me and whispered, "Sami."

I grimaced. He was the only one who called me that.

I wanted so badly to touch him, to feel his hands and mouth on me. If I took the step, everything we'd been through over the past year was meaningless. Nothing would change.

Well, sex was the one thing I wouldn't change. He was the only man whose touch I'd ever known and would always crave. He knew what I wanted and needed before I did. He was the perfect lover.

Too bad the way he was in the bedroom wasn't anything like the man outside it.

He represented conservative values, albeit with a few modern beliefs. He had no tolerance for sensationalism or excess, everything my clients usually projected.

"Give us another chance, baby."

He reached out to cup my face, but I moved out of his way, turning toward the water again.

"Don't. I won't fall back into our pattern."

"We'll do it differently this time."

"Over the last few years, I've believed that too many times, only to see things shatter. I stupidly accepted it when we were in law school, and then I grinned and bore it when we started our careers. I can't do it anymore." I shook my head. "It won't work. I'm going to stay in the limelight. I won't ever be in the shadows again."

"Sami, please."

I pinched the bridge of my nose and then wiped away a stray tear.

"Go home to the condo you got when we separated, Devin James Camden. I'm sure you have a full docket tomorrow. You don't need me to distract you. Besides, if you stay any longer, I'm sure a photographer will see you, and you've made it crystal clear that your privacy and reputation are more important than anything else."

"I'm not giving up." His fingers grazed along the back of my neck. "You're it for me."

"It's over, Devin." My shoulders shook as I dug my nails into my palms. "I've accepted it. Now you have to."

"Not happening." His voice grew cool. "For it to end, we have to divorce, and I will fight you every step of the way."

"Dammit." I whirled around.

He smirked, turning toward the pathway. "I never back down. You should know this. Consider yourself warned."

CHAPTER THREE

A week after my encounter with Devin and the end of my representation of Clint Bassett, I walked toward the doors of my law firm, Kumar, Zain, & Associates.

I'd enjoyed seven days of sleeping in, yoga, and countless laps in the pool. Now it was time to get a little work in so I wouldn't go insane from relaxation. I'd become a workaholic and trying to break the habit had become harder than I thought.

At least I had Karina to keep me up to date with the antics of the Bassetts. Her daily report kept me from getting bored. Thankfully, Karina hadn't thrown her hands up and decided she'd rather work for another firm instead of keeping Clint in line.

I took in the sign above the building, and a slight jolt shot through me. After five years and a few well-known clients, my firm was considered one of the top litigation groups in Washington State.

I'd graduated from law school when most of my friends were finishing up their undergraduate degrees. Besides my best friend, Jacinta, who was a super nerd herself, very few people could say they'd completed law school and clerked for some of the top judges in Texas by the age of twenty-one. A lot of doors opened up when you were the child of Minesh Kumar, a finance and tech billionaire. Thankfully, once I started work and proved my worth, most people forgot my parentage and focused on my skills.

A couple of years later, when I'd moved to Seattle and eventually started my firm, my reputation as a top up-and-coming litigator was all anyone knew about me. To this day, most people had no clue whose daughter I was.

I walked inside and toward the elevator. I punched the button and then I straightened my shirt over my jeans. Rarely would I come to the office so casual, but technically I wasn't working.

As the cab doors closed, I noticed some surprised glances projected in my direction along with a few worried ones.

What could be going on?

I had planned to run in, grab some files I needed to review, and be out the door within minutes, giving me more than enough time to grab some food at my favorite Thai place and get back home for a phone conference with a former client.

Now I was second-guessing this thought process. There was no doubt I'd have to put out some sort of fire.

God. Please don't let it be anything to do with Clint.

I sent my prayers up to heaven and exited the elevator. I turned the corner leading to the executive offices and then came to an abrupt halt.

Devin was in my law partner Tara's office.

All our offices were made of glass walls to give the illusion of openness with the benefit of soundproofing. There was the option to tint the glass for even more privacy, but we rarely used that.

This couldn't be good, no matter what it was. Tara's facial expression told me she was pissed, and Dev's said he was determined to get what he wanted. He'd given me that same stance numerous times over the years.

I approached the door and knocked before opening it.

"Why are you here?" I fixed Dev with a glare.

"I came to get advice on what my options were to live in our house. The condo is small, and I need space to spread out. I think nine thousand square feet is plenty of room to keep us from bumping into each other."

I clenched my jaw, stepping into the office and shutting the door. "You never expressed any inclination or desire to move in. If I recall, you wanted nothing to do with me or the house."

Tears prickled the backs of my eyes as I remembered the devastation I'd felt my first night under the roof of our beautiful home.

"I changed my mind."

"Well, you can change it back."

"Not happening. I have rights. You think Clint Bassett is a pain in your ass, wait until I get started." He lifted a brow. "Are you afraid of us living together again?"

The last thing I needed was him under the same roof as me. We'd end up fucking within the first ten minutes, and we both knew it. I had to keep my head on and my hormones in check.

Plus, I was in the middle of making essential plans I wasn't ready to disclose to Devin.

"Tara, I know this is your office and all. But would you give me a moment alone with Devin James Camden?"

I knew some of the clerks were loitering close by. Only a select few knew about my relationship with Devin, and they were long-term staff who'd all signed non-disclosures.

Without a word, Tara got up and left the office, closing the door behind her.

"Do you know you only call me by my full name when you're irritated with me? No matter how much you like to deny it, you have a true Southern side to you."

I ran a frustrated hand over my face.

"What do you want from me, Dev?"

"Say that again." He stood and walked over to where I leaned against Tara's desk. "Say my name the way you've always done. The way you say it when I make love to you."

He traced my lips with his thumb, making my pulse jump.

I grabbed his hand, planning to push it away, when I noticed his ring, a custom-made gold-and-platinum band.

"Why are you wearing it now? It's been almost five years."

I stared at the ring I'd given him. The one that meant we belonged to each other.

"Because my wife refuses to wear hers unless I wear mine. I want every man in your vicinity to know you belong to me."

I released his hand and tried to move away from him, but he caged me against the desk with an arm on either side of my hips.

"You confuse me. What's changed? You're still a judge who needs to keep a low profile, and I'm an attorney who takes on well-known clients and has become a celebrity in my own right. Hell, I have groupies."

"I thought about what you said last week, about putting you first."

"And?" I folded my arms across my chest.

"I can't lose you. The thought of anyone else touching you…" his fingers gripped my thighs, "…anyone else kissing any part of you…" he sank to the floor, holding my legs tighter, making my core spasm, "…giving you pleasure, is unbearable to fathom. I've spent too many years neglecting you." His thumb grazed the inside of my jean-clad crotch, making a moan form in the back of my throat. "The idea of another man taking my place rips me apart. And I know, without a doubt, we are headed in that direction unless I change."

I glanced to the side and noticed one of my legal secretaries doing her best not to gawk at the sight of Dev kneeling before me, with his face a hairsbreadth from my overheated sex.

"Dev, stand up. Everyone will know we were involved if you don't stop this."

"Are involved."

I couldn't bring myself to repeat him. Sexual attraction couldn't be the only thing to make a relationship.

Devin kissed the inside of my knee. "We're married. That's as involved as a couple gets."

He gazed up at me, and I held in the urge to grip his hair and make him kiss my feet for all the crap he'd made me deal with throughout our time together.

"It's not that simple. If you recall, you're the one who wanted to keep our relationship quiet for our careers' sake. How do we go from pretending we barely know each other to a normal married couple? Besides, my life is going to get a hell of a lot more complicated before it settles down again."

A look passed in his eyes, telling me I shouldn't have said that.

Only a few people knew what I was considering. And if Devin latched on, he wouldn't let go until he knew everything.

To my surprise, he only responded with, "By walking out that door, hand in hand."

At that moment, Tara barged in, shaking her head at seeing Devin on his knees between my legs. She'd known about my relationship with Devin from the time she and I were in law school together, and nothing surprised her when it came to our antics. She was also the one who drafted the separation decree I'd sent to Devin six weeks ago.

"Sam, we've got a big problem. I truly regret pushing that damn case onto you."

Dev released my hips, stood, and let me slip around him.

"What happened?" I asked a little too breathlessly, giving away the intimacy of what she'd interrupted.

"Look outside."

Both Dev and I walked over to the sixth-story window.

There were at least fifty photographers and media outlets outside the building with people holding signs saying "Hot Stuff," and police officers trying to keep the crowd under control.

"They weren't there twenty minutes ago. What happened?"

"Your former client announced on his show that he was on a mission to get you laid. He decided that he wanted to play radio matchmaker, offering one million dollars to the lucky man he approved to take you out."

"Oh, for the love of God."

I released a deep breath as I willed away the painful throb flaring to life in my head.

"Tara, go see if you can call in more security. I'll get to the bottom of this from my end."

I ignored Dev's pacing as I reached for my phone and dialed Clint Bassett's private number.

"Yello, sexy lady. What can I do you for?"

"Clint, you have to stop this. My life is crazy enough. I

thought you accepted my decision. Why would you create this contest? I am not dating anyone you pick."

"It's either I find you a date or nominate you for president. I think you'd make a fabulous politician, all controlled exterior but a heart that bleeds for any injustice."

"Clint, please."

"I did this for you, Sam." Clint's voice went from the cocky radio DJ to the normal and ultra-private man outside of the media. "The guy that's had you twisted up for the last few months needs a kick in the ass. Especially if you're about to do what I suspect you're about to do."

How the hell would he know my plans when I hadn't made anything official?

Before I could respond, he spoke again. "And don't try to deny that you have a man. I'm going to make him see red in order to fix things with you."

"I appreciate the thought, but this is the worst way to go about it. I don't need this type of drama added to my life."

"Sure, you do."

"Clint..." I couldn't hide my irritation.

"Sam."

"Why don't you terrorize Karina instead of me?"

"Because that battle-ax is scarier than my Italian grandmother with a cast-iron skillet."

I started laughing, and I couldn't help it.

A throat cleared behind me, bringing me back to the situation at hand.

"He's there, isn't he?"

"I have no idea what you're talking about."

"Good. I'll be up in a second. I want to see the man who made me lose the best damn attorney I've ever encountered." Clint hung up before I could respond.

Oh shit, this was about to go from bad to worse.

"Dev, can we talk later? Clint is on his way up, and I need to handle this."

"No." His gaze bored into mine. "I'd like to meet the man who thinks my wife needs a date."

"You can't get possessive when for the last six years of our relationship, you pretended to date other women and never cared what man was around me."

"I've always been possessive of you. Do you think I liked seeing my woman on another man's arm? Why do you think I fucked your brains out the minute you got home?"

My cheeks flushed as memories of past encounters flooded my mind.

"That was your choice, not mine."

"From now on the only man you're seen with is me."

"It doesn't work that way. You don't get to dictate what I do. I've let you steamroll me for too long, and it stops now."

"Is that right?"

I crossed my arms in front of me. "Did I stutter?"

"Listen carefully, Mrs. Camden."

"Ms. Kumar," I countered. "That's my professional name."

He walked forward, making me retreat until my back hit the wall. He cupped the back of my head while the other gripped my waist.

"You may be the boss here, but when we're together we both know who's in charge, and it isn't you."

My heartbeat accelerated, and my breath came out a little shallow.

"Then it's time things changed. It doesn't work anymore."

"Is that so?" He pressed his hard cock against my abdomen.

"Yes."

"Liar. I bet if I slipped my hand down your pants, I'd find you aroused and soaked for me."

I licked my lips, and his eyes went to them, dilating.

Before he could lean down and kiss me, I heard from behind him, "Well hell. A federal judge and a high-profile attorney. Now it makes complete sense why you ditched me. You two send conflict of interest to a whole new level."

A flash of annoyance crossed Dev's face as he held my gaze. "We'll continue this discussion later."

He kissed my forehead in the way it always made me melt, and released his hold on me.

Turning to Clint, he extended his hand. "Mr. Bassett."

"Judge Camden." Clint shook his hand and inclined his head. "So, are you two dating or is it more?"

He noticed the ring on Dev's left hand.

"You could say that. She's my wife."

Clint gave no outward reaction to Devin's

announcement except his signature smirk.

"Well, you've done a piss-poor job of keeping her happy. I know when a woman spends her time alone and crying. I've raised four daughters. I suggest fixing whatever is wrong between you two. Within minutes of my announcement, I had thousands of applications flood the station inbox for the opportunity to take your place. She needs a good man by her side."

I groaned out loud and smacked the back of my head against the wall I leaned on.

Dev clenched his jaw. "I'm not the one being sued by my ex-wife."

"True, but I'm on the side you'll be on soon enough. I neglected Kim for years and then she turned to someone else. The divorce was a hair-trigger reaction to my pain. Something I'll regret for the rest of my life."

Clint had never expressed his remorse until this moment. I knew he'd been devastated when he learned of Kim's affair. He'd drawn first blood by calling her out on national radio. Before that day, he'd never once discussed his twenty-year marriage. Now he was in a heated lawsuit that had nothing to do with the money at stake and everything to do with the pain.

"Your advice is duly noted, Mr. Bassett." Dev flashed me a grin. "I'll see you tonight when I move in."

"Wait. What? You can't be serious." I braced myself against the windowsill.

"Either that or I sue to have access to a house that is fifty percent mine. You make the call."

CHAPTER FOUR

"Samina, have you seen the news?" my friend Sarah asked the second I answered the phone.

She was Nathan Travis's wife and one of Seattle's top surgeons who happened to be the granddaughter of a former president and a connoisseur of all things news.

If she didn't know about it, then most likely it didn't happen. She had such a busy schedule between Nathan, their kids, and her practice that I didn't know when she found time to keep up with current events.

She apparently forgot or conveniently ignored my text from earlier in the day, where I specifically said not to call so I could mentally prepare for Devin to move in.

I poured myself a cup of coffee and set the French press on the warmer. "No. I unplugged. Remember?"

The last thing I wanted to do was get on any form of media after what I'd dealt with at the office today.

Clint's radio mission had turned my life into even more

of a spectacle, forcing me to use Tara's car and the private garage exit to leave the building. By the time I arrived home, the groups of paparazzi outside my house had grown so much that part of my street had to be shut down.

Thankfully the sheriff's department had forced the media to leave the area and camp out at the entrance of my residential community.

"Well, future senator. I suggest you get plugged in."

I winced. Why had I told her what I was planning?

Because her whole life has been about politics and her mother is the current Secretary of State. She's the only one who can give it to you straight.

"I don't care," I said. "Can you top having my former client tell my estranged husband to fix my marriage or he was going to find me another man?"

"Yes. If a bailiff found said client having sex with his ex-wife in a courthouse bathroom. He acted like it was no big deal when he spoke to the reporters later."

I felt heat and anger creep up my face. This could not be happening. Four months of my life and they end up back together?

"I'm going to wring his neck the next time I see him."

"It's been a very active news day."

"That means you're leaving something out. Spill it." I sat on one of the barstools lining the island.

"He credited his visit to your office today as the inspiration for wanting to reconcile with his wife."

Sure, my husband threatening to sue me to live in our house was going to trigger thoughts of happily ever after.

"And?" I probed.

"He's now more determined than ever to find you a date. With the help of Kimberly, of course."

I groaned and then rested my head on the hard granite in front of me.

"Of course. That's all I need. The woman who called me Clint's tramp and whore is going to play matchmaker. Someone kill me now."

"It could be worse."

"I doubt that. My career as an attorney is tanked. I've gone from being the take-no-one's-shit bulldog litigator to a contestant on a dating game orchestrated by a former client."

"It's not as if this is your first high-profile case. You've represented at least three politicians and a swarm of TV and movie celebrities. Remember Debbie?"

My neighbor Debbie was my first politically connected client. She'd discovered through a tabloid reporter that she was the secret love child of two senators who were in opposing parties and married to other people.

"Yes, but she and everyone else I've represented avoided any and all media whenever possible. Clint caters to them. His ratings depend on them. I'm collateral damage."

"I think you're too sensitive."

"Sarah, this case put the final nail in the coffin of my marriage. Now I'm left to make plans for a future without the one person I've always loved."

"What did you expect? Great sex doesn't make a stable

marriage. Every time things got difficult, instead of working it out, you would ignore the situation and try to fix the problems by having sex for hours on end or go on vacation where you'd fuck as if your life depended on it."

The one place where Dev and I had no problem communicating was in the bedroom. We could read each other without any difficulties, and getting it on like rabbits was our way of dealing with the frustration of our dueling careers.

The moment I took on Clint as a client and he threw me into the national spotlight, Devin and I couldn't mask our issues anymore.

I wanted the support I'd given him during his rise through the ranks and eventually to a position as federal judge, and he wanted things to remain the same.

It was when life became too hard for him to handle that we ultimately separated.

"You're right. Something had to give, and neither of us was going to budge."

"Do you miss him?"

"Yes. Of course, I do," I responded without hesitation. He held a piece of my heart that I'd never get back whether we stayed together or not.

"Do you have any hope of fixing things?"

"I never gave up hope."

"But?"

"But, it has to be different if we are going to salvage our relationship. I refuse to be a secret anymore. This was not how I planned to spend the first years of my marriage. Do you know what it was like to watch Dev get sworn in from the audience instead of by his side like all the other judges' wives?

"Yes, he's a politician's son, but I'm the daughter of a freaking billionaire. I stood up to my father when he disapproved of us. Devin never did that for me. His parents still don't know we're married. I moved thousands of miles away from Texas, from my family and a successful, cushy future, to be with him. I deserve better."

I gasped for a few deep breaths as my temper flared and tears prickled my eyes. "I'm done living for other people. First it was for my father, then it was for Devin. Besides, I'm about to use my fame to catapult me to a new phase of life that Devin will never be able to handle. He's told me countless times how he wished his father would give up politics."

I rarely discussed the hurt I felt about my marriage with anyone. I was ashamed of putting myself in this position. Even Dev's sister and my best friend thought I was a moron for how I'd allowed him to treat me. She'd wanted me to leave Devin years ago.

"Feel better, now that you got that off your chest? I expected you to explode months ago."

I could almost envision the smirk on her face as she said that.

This was her plan. To get me to release the frustration and anger.

"Yes. You're such an ass."

"Takes one to know one. Seriously, I wouldn't worry

about your marriage staying a secret for long. The moment you file the candidacy paperwork for US Senate, nothing about you is going to remain quiet."

I shifted the phone to my other ear and pinched the bridge of my nose. "I know."

"The paps are going to have a field day when they discover that you had a secret wedding four years ago to ultra-conservative Louisiana Senator Richard Camden's eldest son."

"I never hid it. I just never acknowledged it in public."

"Answered like a true politician."

"Whatever," I mumbled as I pressed the speaker button, then set the phone on the counter and took a sip of my coffee.

"How do you think your parents will react to the news you're running for Senate?"

Great, something else to worry about. Sarah was full of happy thoughts today.

"Papa is going to lose his mind when the press starts hounding him. I doubt this will lead to a family reconciliation. He is all about donating to both sides of the aisle and using those associations to his benefit. Having a child enter the political game instead of business will be insulting to everything he believed he put into his children's upbringing, even from me the black sheep of the family."

"Oh, come on. My parents would be so thrilled if I jumped into politics, especially against that jackass

Anthony Sanders. That man is a no-good, double-talking, sexist piece of shit."

I almost asked her to tell me how she truly felt about my future opponent but decided against it. If Sarah got on her soapbox, it could be an hour before she came up for air.

"Yes, but that's your quote-unquote family business." I air-quoted my words with my fingers. "Remember when I told you how Papa reacted the day he found out Ashur joined the Air Force?"

"You said he was livid and tried to use his connections to stop Ash from enlisting."

"Well, that would be mild compared to a child entering politics. At least most of his influence is in Texas and doesn't reach to Washington State."

"What about your mom and brother?"

"She supports me unconditionally and Ash already knows about my plans. I told him what I was preparing to do when he came up for a client meeting. The second I tell him I filed, he's going to start contacting donors."

Ashur was the one person I had no doubt would stand behind me in anything I pursued.

"And Devin's parents? They're about to get a double whammy—not only is their son married, but their daughter-in-law is going to be the politician."

I sighed. "Well, once they get over the shock of finding out about Devin and me, their reaction won't be any better than my father's. No, that's not true. Dev's mom will support me. She is all about women entering the congressional ring. Dev's dad is the one who'll go ballistic.

The good senator will view it as a slap in the face. Dev was supposed to follow in his footsteps and become part of the next generation of Louisiana senators. When Dev decided to become a judge, Senator Camden's plans for his son's future changed to him someday holding a seat on the United States Supreme Court."

I could almost see the shock and anger on both our fathers' faces.

"Sorry I brought it up. I never meant to upset you."

"It's okay. I have to face the facts of any political bid I consider."

"I hate to break it to you, but you have something more important to worry about. Your estranged husband is going to move into the mansion you built together. You better figure out where he's going to sleep, and it better not be with you."

I ignored the warning in her voice.

"Thanks, Sarah. I can always count on you to prioritize my stress."

"Samina, if you want it to change, you can't jump into bed together."

"We haven't slept together for at least six weeks." I crossed my arms and frowned at the phone, then realized she couldn't see me.

"Umm. Correct me if I'm wrong, but haven't you been separated for over four months? Why were you bumping uglies, and why am I finding out now?"

I cringed. No one knew about that night but Dev and me. He'd come to the house to check on the progress of the pool and found me sleeping on a lounger by the beach. When he tried to wake me, I thought I was having a vivid dream and grabbed him, pulling him toward me. Then, as always, we ended up having crazy monkey sex.

"Yeah, about that. Let's say it won't happen again anytime soon. The next morning, Dev assumed we were back to normal, and for me, nothing had changed. Which, in turn, led to an epic fight and resulted in him flying home to Louisiana to take that bitch Veronica to the Mardi Gras ball his grandparents throw every year."

"Bitter much?"

"You have no idea," I grumbled, trying to push back the hurt bubbling up.

That was the day I'd made my decision to take control of my life. A man who claimed to love me but couldn't make me a priority didn't deserve me in his life.

"Sam, you can't do the same thing over and over and expect the outcome to be different."

"I know, Sarah. I'll try my best."

"Do or do not. There is no try."

I rolled my eyes. "Yes, Yoda. You and the kids have been watching too many *Star Wars* marathons."

"You were on my couch for seven of the nine movies." She paused to say something to a person in the room with her. "Hey, I have to go. You know, the mom thing. Samina, I love you. Be good."

"Yes, Jedi Master."

Sarah laughed before she said, "Bye, young Padawan."

I hung up the phone and couldn't help but smile. We were such dorks.

Grabbing a sweater and blanket, I headed for the outdoor sofas near the fire pit. I ignited the fire and then made myself comfortable on the cushions.

I closed my eyes as the cool summer breeze from the Sound glided over my face, and the heat from the burning lava rocks warmed the rest of me.

This was my respite before the storm.

I'd never bar Dev from his own house, but I couldn't help but worry about what to expect.

Could we live under the same roof again? I wasn't the same Samina who'd accepted being second to his aspirations.

I wanted it all or nothing.

I released a deep yawn and snuggled under the covers.

If I stayed here long enough, I could fall asleep. Maybe a short catnap was in order. Then I'd have the energy to handle the emotions of having Dev under the same roof as me again.

"Now this reminds me of another time, not so long ago, but you were naked under the blanket."

CHAPTER FIVE

My breath hitched as I took in Devin leaning against the pergola that shaded the pool. He no longer wore his suit but instead a pair of well-worn jeans and a fitted black T-shirt. His sandy-brown hair was messy as if he'd run his fingers through it.

He peered at me with such intensity that butterflies tickled my stomach. I'd had the same reaction the first time we met. Years later, he'd claimed I was his from that first glance. And I couldn't deny the truth of his statement.

Devin held my gaze as he moved to the couch and sat where my feet were, picking them up and placing them on his lap.

"I'm home," he said and started to massage my feet.

I tried to pull my feet away, but he gripped them tight.

"We can't pretend the last four months didn't happen."

"I can't change the past, Sami. It's time to focus on our future."

I pushed out of his hold and sat up. "I'm not doing this again. I'm not going to sweep it under the rug. I want it all, Devin James Camden, or nothing. I'll never be your dirty little secret again."

"I've never thought of you that way."

"Are you fucking kidding me? Your parents don't know anything about me, except that I am your sister's best friend from law school. I get that they wanted you to marry someone from their social circle in Louisiana but did you ever think it was the same for me?"

I stood and paced, then paused to watch the flames of the fire.

My father expected me to pick someone out of an approved list of men who had an impeccable pedigree and affluent family. A man who came from the same culture and background. I'd accepted the traditional plan for my life until the day I'd met my roommate's brother. Devin rocked my acceptance of family rules and traditions to the core. For him, I turned my back on everything I ever knew.

"I told them."

I whirled around to face him, not believing what he said.

"What did you tell them? Do they know we're married? Or am I some girl you're seeing?"

"They know you're my wife. Dad said they knew before I ever decided to tell them."

There was only one person I could think of who would get pleasure from revealing our secret.

"Papa told them."

Devin nodded. "Apparently they've known since right after our honeymoon."

"I don't understand. Why didn't your parents say anything?"

"Because our fathers thought we were going through a phase and would break up. They were hoping we'd get an annulment so everyone could pretend we didn't exist." There was a tinge of anger in his words.

"I don't believe either of our mothers was involved. My mom has been my buffer since Papa found out we were dating. And yours has been kind to me from the beginning when Jacinta and I were roommates in law school. To this day, she calls me every week to check up on me and hear about the escapades of my clients."

"I didn't know she did that."

"Dev. We've barely spent any time together in the last year and a half. And when we are together, we're arguing, or we're..." I trailed off and faced the fire.

He finished my statement. "Fucking."

I nodded.

The need for him lingered constantly.

"Why did you decide now was the time to tell your parents?"

"After you kicked me off the property last week I did a lot of thinking. I know you moved to Seattle and retook the bar for me. You did a lot for me over the years. Sami, I never wanted you to feel you were second to what I wanted."

Devin stood, moving behind me, and then gripped my shoulders, pulling me back against his chest.

I wanted to relax into his hold, but I held myself stiff.

"I was second. I've never been a priority for you. If I were important, you would never have let me go to functions and parties with someone else or have taken another woman out for the image of it, and most of all you would have had me standing next to you when you were sworn in."

"That's not fair. I never did anything with any of them. You're the one I'd come and lose myself in."

I shoved out of his arms.

"Is it fair knowing the man you loved kept you a secret from his family, that his career aspirations came before yours? Or that he never wanted to be seen in public with you for fear of how a non-Caucasian, liberal attorney wife would affect his father's reelection chances in his extremely conservative state of Louisiana? What sucks is I'm not even a liberal. Why did you marry me if you're so ashamed of who I am?"

Tears poured down my cheeks. Through all our fights, I'd never asked that question.

I was such an idiot.

Dev cupped my face. "Because I love you. I couldn't see my life with anyone but you. I am anything but ashamed of you."

"No. You don't get to say that and expect everything to be okay."

"Don't you think I know this?" He stepped away from

me and ran a frustrated hand through his hair. "I fucked up. I'd hate any man who'd do the same thing to my sister. I get why Ashur hates me."

My big brother took overprotective to a whole new level, and anyone he perceived as hurting me, even one of his closest friends, was enemy number one.

Dev couldn't take all the blame for this mess.

"I fucked up too. Do you want to know who I'm angry with the most? It's me. I'm a strong, independent woman and I let my love for you push my needs behind yours. I made it okay for you to cater to your family and your job."

"How are we going to fix this, Sami? You want to fix this, don't you?"

The uncertainty in his voice broke my heart. He was the most confident man I knew.

I had to harden myself against him, or I'd never stop the repeated pattern of our relationship.

"I don't know if it's possible if things don't change."

"So that's not a no. There is still a chance?"

I released a deep breath. I'd always believed I'd get married once and for the rest of my life. With everything I'd strengthened myself against over the past few months, I'd never stopped hoping. Could I do this? He was asking me to help fix the mess we made. My answer would determine our next steps.

Before I lost my nerve, I said, "Yes."

Relief washed over his face, and then after a few seconds, a grin appeared.

"I have a plan."

He always had a plan. This would be good.

I lifted a brow and waited.

"There is only one way to make sure you never have any doubt about how I feel about you, that I'm not ashamed of us, of you. It's something I've wanted to do for a long time."

He walked toward me with a glint in his eyes that made me retreat.

"And what's that?"

"To have a baby."

He couldn't be serious.

"Say that again." I continued my retreat until my calves grazed the stone surrounding the fire pit.

"I want us to have a baby."

Devin gripped my waist and pulled me toward him.

My heartbeat accelerated. I hated when Dev looked at me like I was the center of his world.

I broke his spell on me by slipping out of his hold and moving to the couch.

"Are you out of your mind? A baby isn't going to solve the problems between us."

"What is more proof that I am committed to us than wanting a baby?"

I growled. "You're such a man! I will not bring a child into this situation when all we do is argue."

"We do more than argue, Sami."

"If you want to prove to me I'm a priority, then be seen in public with me, let your colleagues know you're married, don't keep me on the sidelines. To any other man, I'd be the catch of the century. Who doesn't want a Stanford-educated attorney who happens to be an heiress to a billion-dollar fortune?"

"Is that an ultimatum?"

"Yes, like the one you gave me six weeks ago. I want it all, or we end it now. I'd rather have a broken heart and live alone than with you and be half the person I should be."

His gaze bored into mine, but he didn't say anything in response. I refused to look away. He would not win this one, no matter how he affected me.

"Fine," he said, turning away from me. "Get changed. We're going out."

He moved toward the house.

"What?"

I sat there in a daze. Dev's change in mood was giving me whiplash.

"You heard me." He paused at the terrace doors. "I'm taking my wife out to dinner."

He'd lost his mind.

"Right now?"

"Yes, now," he said without looking in my direction, and then stepped into the sunroom.

I blew out a frustrated breath and followed him inside.

"You do realize the second we pass through the gates, the paparazzi are going to be on us?"

"That's the point." He grabbed the bags he'd dropped by the base of the stairs and began to climb. "You've got fifteen minutes. I suggest you hurry."

"Dammit, Dev." I stomped up the stairs after him. "Hold on a minute. The guest rooms are that way."

I pointed to the other side of the landing.

He turned so fast I collided with his chest. He glowered down at me, making my five- two frame seem microscopic compared to his six-foot-one.

"Let me make this clear, Samina mine. I am sleeping in my bedroom."

"You'll be alone then. I'll move to another room."

"You won't be alone. Where you sleep, I sleep."

He gave me a breathtaking smile that made me want to jump him and punch him at the same time.

"No."

"Yes."

"Then I guess you'll be sleeping on the floor of the living room because I'd rather sleep on the couch and there isn't enough room for you." I jerked my chin.

He smirked in response and said, "If you decide to sleep on the couch, I'll be right there behind you or under you. If you recall, we had it custom made to fit both of us."

Damn, if only the designer hadn't made the suggestion.

"Fine, we'll sleep in the bedroom," I growled. "But don't think for a second that I'm having sex with you."

He ran a finger over my bottom lip. "I didn't say anything about sex."

I clenched my jaw, shoved past him, and went straight for my closet.

I threw off my sweater and pushed down my jeans. I

rummaged through the racks, trying to figure out what to wear.

I grabbed a strapless summer dress and a light cardigan. Laying both on the chaise in the center of my closet, I reached behind me to take off my bra and quickly slipped on my dress.

As I reached for the zipper in the back of my dress, I felt Dev's hands.

"I'll do it. Lift your hair." His voice was rough, making me realize he'd watched me change.

Goosebumps prickled my skin as he zipped my dress, and I almost let out a groan. The wetness pooling between my legs added to the constant throbbing I felt whenever he was around.

"Are you cold?"

"No."

I refused to turn around. My body ached for Dev's touch, and this little bit of familiarity made me want to beg him for more.

I took a deep breath and moved into the bathroom.

As I started to apply my lipstick, I noticed Dev standing against one of the walls, watching me with lust in his eyes. There was also a distinct bulge in his pants.

"Do you remember the last time we were in here together?"

How could I forget?

We'd come to inspect the house a month before our move-in date and ended in the master bathroom looking over the newly installed tile, and before I understood what was happening, Dev pushed me against the marble counter and had his way with me while we watched each other in the mirror.

"No."

He smirked. "Want me to remind you?"

"No." My cheeks heated.

He stepped behind me, pressing his hard cock against my back.

"Are you sure? Your shallow breath and flushed face tells me you remember every detail of what happened."

God, what was he doing to me? This man turned me into a panting, soaking mess.

His hands went to the curve of my upper thighs, and he slowly bunched my dress upward. "Are you wet for me, Sami?" he crooned into my ear.

Just when his fingers grazed the edge of my thong, reality set in and I stopped him from going further.

"Dev, we can't do this."

His eyes held mine. The desire staring at me made me want to forget everything I was trying to do.

"Yes, we can." His hand flexed under mine. "We're married."

"No sex. We can't fuck our way out of our problems."

A frown crossed his face, and he stepped away.

"Fine. I'll meet you downstairs."

He tugged his shirt over his head to reveal his hard, sculpted body underneath. One that made me think of all the dirty, naughty things I wanted to do to it.

He paused, smirked over his shoulder, and then walked into his closet.

Bastard. He'd done that on purpose.

"NOT BAD FOR OUR FIRST PUBLIC DATE IN FIVE YEARS." Dev offered me his arm, and I slipped mine into his.

I smiled up at him as he kissed my forehead. "I couldn't agree more."

We'd left our community in my neighbor Debbie's SUV so no one would suspect Dev and I were in the back.

Debbie had driven us around for an extra twenty minutes before she dropped us off near Dev's office, where we took his car the rest of the way.

After a short drive out of the Seattle area, we relaxed and enjoyed our evening. I'd decided to stop overthinking things and see if it was possible to go out like a normal couple again.

We went to one of our favorite hole-in-the-wall seafood places and ate until our stomachs felt like exploding. No one seemed to pay attention to us, and if they did, they kept it quiet.

It was almost like it had been when we'd first met. Before the high-powered careers and all the secrets. I hadn't laughed so much in what seemed like years.

At first, it had felt awkward. We'd barely spent time together in eighteen months, and when we were together, they were outings to vacation spots nowhere near Seattle and usually filled with nonstop sex.

Tonight, once we got over the initial uneasiness, it was natural and carefree.

Dev wasn't the stiff Southern judge who went by the book, and I didn't have to pretend I was the ball-busting Texas transplant.

"You realize this isn't going to last?"

Reporters were sneaky, and you never knew when they might jump out from a hiding spot. Right after Clint had first referred to me as "Hot Stuff" and threw me to his fans, a reporter pretending to be a patient had followed me into my gynecologist's office. Awkward was an understatement when the male reporter realized where he was scheduled for a pap smear.

"Don't jinx us. Once the public finds out, neither of us will be left alone."

I stopped to look up at him. "Dev, are you going to be okay with it? Your father is going to go ballistic."

"His opinion has no bearing on us."

I wanted to argue but kept my mouth shut. I had enough on my plate to add Devin's issues with his father.

"Now I'm taking you home and planning to score."

Arousal shot through my core.

"No, you're not. I meant it. Sex is off the table. We have to work out our issues without letting our hormones cloud our judgment. After we figure out if we can work, then we'll move to intimacy."

"My judgment is crystal clear. You're it for me. End of

story. And watching you come around my cock has always been the highlight of my day."

I rolled my eyes. "You sound like a caveman who has laid claim to his mate."

"When it comes to you, I am one. And I claimed you the day I popped your cherry."

"You make it sound so romantic."

"It was one of the best damn days of my life. The woman I loved agreed to marry me and then gave me a gift only I will ever have in this lifetime."

"I should have made you work for it. It was too easy for you."

He stopped midstep and turned to me. "Easy is not how I remember it. We waited three years."

"Oh please, I was barely legal when we first met. I'd had no idea what kind of horndog I'd gotten involved with. Besides, it's not like you were sexually frustrated the entire time. We did a lot of other stuff."

A mischievous grin touched his face. "We did perfect your oral skills."

"Come on before someone overhears us." I pulled him toward his car, a Porsche 911.

Just as he opened the passenger door, a man approached us. Immediately Dev stepped in front of me, blocking me from view, and I did my best not to cringe. I had to get ahold of my reaction. People would come at me from all sides when I made my political ambitions public.

"Judge Camden, is that Samina Kumar? Is she your date?"

"Yes" was all he said as he helped me get into the car.

"Isn't it a breach of conduct to date an attorney whom you may preside over?"

I grimaced and saw Dev clench his jaw.

He shut the door and moved to his side.

As he opened his door, the reporter rephrased the question.

"Wouldn't it be considered unethical to date someone you may see in your courtroom?"

"Dev don't answer him," I urged him. I'd learned if you gave them any info they'd keep hounding you.

Of course, he ignored me and spoke. "There is nothing unethical or in breach of conduct with my relationship with Ms. Kumar. If you'd done your research before jumping to conclusions, you'd be aware that I would never preside over any of her cases. I have it on record that Ms. Kumar and I have a personal relationship."

This was news to me. I'd have to remember to ask him about it later.

Dev slid into the driver's seat.

"One more question."

I groaned inside and gave Dev an "I told you so" look.

"Who is Ms. Kumar to you? Is she a date set up by Clint Bassett? Or have you been seeing each other for a while?"

Dev contemplated for a second and then turned to the reporter.

"Samina Kumar is Samina Camden. My wife."

CHAPTER SIX

I gawked at Devin. I couldn't believe his answer to the reporter.

He'd outed us. He voluntarily placed himself in the path of public scrutiny.

"Stop staring at me like that," Dev said as he pulled out of the parking space. "I told you that I'm committed."

"I...I don't know what to think. In a matter of weeks, we went from arguing about making this a real marriage to you announcing that I'm your wife. I feel like I'm in a parallel universe."

"For the record, this has always been a real marriage."

The phone rang on the Bluetooth connection on the Porsche's console. It was Dev's mom.

"I think the cat's out of the bag," I said.

"That was fast. We left the reporter less than five minutes ago. You answer. The car is connected to your phone."

I couldn't hide my surprise. He loved the car. We'd always draw straws to see who got to take the sports car to work. Then after I'd decided to separate, I'd left the car in his office garage for him to pick up. It was too painful to be in it without thinking of him.

"You never drove the car after I left it for you in the garage?"

"I didn't see the point. I didn't have you to fight with over it." He shrugged his shoulders. "Answer the call. We'll talk about how real our marriage is later."

I touched a button on the display to answer.

"Hello."

"Samina dear, how are you?" A beautiful Southern Belle accent came over the car's speakers.

"I'm good, Mrs. Camden."

"I think it's time you weren't so formal with me. After all, you're married to Devin. Call me Carol, if not mom."

"Umm...don't you want an explanation?"

She seemed too calm for my comfort.

"Dev told me how he kept it a secret for his and his father's careers. I love my son, but he can be so stupid sometimes. Men want to have their cake and eat it too. My question to you is, why did you put up with it? You're a smart, successful woman. How could you do that to yourself? My son can't be that good in bed."

My eyes nearly bugged out of my head. If she only knew.

"Mom, I'm on the line. You're on the car speaker."

"I know, sweetheart. A reporter just called to inform

me you're out and about and then to ask my opinion of your relationship with liberal attorney Samina Kumar."

Both Dev and I cringed.

Dev spoke before I could. "What did you say?"

"Well, I told them it was rude to call an unlisted number without permission and then I said Samina isn't a liberal, she's an independent. You know how these reporters are, twisting the facts."

"Mom," Dev grumbled.

She ignored him and spoke to me. "Samina, I hope you don't mind, but I told them to leave my daughter-in-law alone."

"No, I don't mind. I'm sorry the reporter bothered you."

"It was nothing. I deal with worse on a regular basis. I can't believe that nosy man called you a liberal. Do you remember all those debates you and Jacinta would get into in your apartment when I'd visit? I paid attention. I'm more liberal than you are on certain matters."

"Mom, focus."

"Devin James Camden, I don't know how people mistake you for a Southern gentleman. You are as rude as a toddler who thinks his toy is stolen. I have no idea where I went wrong."

I started laughing. Conversations with Mrs. Camden... Carol, were always like this.

She was one of the kindest women I'd ever met. She loved with all her heart, and if she took you into her circle, you were hers for life.

In public, she portrayed the always-poised Southern lady who never was fazed by the ups and downs of being married to a politician. But in private, she was a force when riled. Even the formidable Richard Camden was afraid of his wife's temper on the rare occasions when it appeared.

"He has certain charms that make us want to keep him around." I laughed up at Dev.

"Hilarious, ladies." His hand moved to my thigh and inched upward but stopped when I clamped my thighs to keep him from going further. "I'm glad I'm here to humor you."

My pulse accelerated, and my nipples hardened to stiff peaks.

Dammit. Why did his slightest touch affect me?

"You've always been good for a laugh, Dev honey. Now for the real reason I called."

"Are you saying you lied, Mom, and the reporter story was a ruse?"

"Leave her alone, Dev," I said.

"I'm used to him, Samina. What I wanted to say was you two need to come to Jacinta's Fourth of July party on the river. She's chartered a riverboat to sail the Colorado River to watch the fireworks."

Ever since Jacinta had moved to Austin to pursue her law practice and possible political career, she'd thrown an annual party. She loved to say a little bit of liquor mixed with apple pie opened the purse strings.

I wanted to go, but with everything going on with my

case, not to mention Devin, I'd declined Jacinta's invitation.

"We'll be there. Sami and I'll take a flight out this Thursday."

He squeezed my leg again and somehow moved higher.

"No," I said through a breathless whisper as I tried to pull his fingers away, but he reached the center of my soaked underwear.

He *tsk*ed in my direction and returned his gaze to the road.

"I'm so happy you two will be there. We're driving down on Wednesday. Your father wants to get in early to reconnect with some old friends."

I gasped and then held in a moan as Dev touched my clit and a spasm shot through my core.

Embarrassment hit me as I realized Dev's mom had heard me.

I smacked Dev's hand, which only made him push past my minuscule thong and rim my dripping pussy.

I threw my head back and bit my lips to keep in the orgasm about to erupt.

"Devin James, you better not be doing what I think you're doing."

"I have no idea what you're talking about," he responded as his thumb started a rhythm that would send me over.

"Leave her alone and concentrate on driving. I expect a teenager to be a constant horndog, but you're thirty-five.

Let go of her and put both hands on that wheel. Don't you have any self-control?"

I wanted to protest. I was almost there, but Dev followed orders and pulled his hand from between my legs, licked his fingers clean, and then grabbed the steering wheel.

"When it comes to Sami, I have none."

I closed my eyes and tried to calm my body.

Dammit, I wasn't supposed to do anything sexual with him. Now my body was on fire. He knew every button to push, and my clit was screaming for some attention.

"Devin, when you get to Texas, we're going to have a very serious conversation. One where you won't be able to talk your way out of the hole you're in."

"I hear you, Mom."

I lifted my head and glanced at Dev, giving him a "what was that about?" look.

"Samina dear, I look forward to seeing you. And maybe if my son gets his head out of his ass, you'll give me a grandbaby one of these days."

She hung up before I could respond.

"If I had my way, you'd be pregnant this very minute."

"Until an hour ago, no one knew we were together. What was I going to be, your secret baby mama with your secret child? No thanks."

"We are together, Sami. And I'd never hide our child from the world."

"Excuse me if I don't believe you."

Clenching his jaw, Dev paused the car at the entrance

of our property and nodded to the security guard stationed on our driveway. He waved us through, but not before a reporter caught sight of us and a barrage of lights flashed all around us.

I'd encountered a few of these reporters before and slid down from my seat, doing everything to be invisible.

"They know you're with me, Sami. There's no point in hiding."

I ignored him and stayed in the cramped space on the floorboard until we reached our garage. He didn't know what one reporter could do. I'd dealt with it for over four months. This crowd was tame compared to what happened right after Clint had hired me.

You have to get it together, Samina. This is only the beginning.

"Sami? What's going on?"

"I'm okay. Just give me a minute."

I will not let them win. I will not let them win.

"Baby. You're crying."

The second he parked the car and the garage door closed, he jumped out and ran to my side. Opening the door, he crouched in front of me.

"It's going to be okay," he crooned as he pulled me toward him.

I refused to move from my spot and rested my forehead against the smooth leather of the seat.

"What happened? Tell me what's going on."

"They stalk you and tear apart your life. They laugh when they invade your private moments."

He stroked my hair. "They get paid to take the pictures."

I was going to have to tell him, or he wasn't going to understand this was beyond a photograph.

"Does getting paid make it okay to break into the house and take pictures of you in the shower?"

His gaze bored into mine. "What the hell are you talking about?"

"One of the reporters out there broke into our house. I have a restraining order against him, but it doesn't look like he cares that he is within the prohibited area."

"Why didn't I know about this?"

Tears trailed down my face.

Besides Tara, Jacinta, and my brother, I'd kept the incident as quiet as possible.

I inhaled deep and opened my lips to explain.

"Sami baby, not here. Let's go inside. I'll make you a drink, and then we can talk."

I nodded and allowed him to help me out of the car.

Once we entered the house, Dev had me sit on the bench in the mudroom, removed my shoes, and before I could protest, lifted me up and carried me into the living room.

He sat me on the couch and moved to the bar in the back of the room. As he fixed our drinks, I opened my phone and brought up the pictures. I hated looking at them. It was at my weakest point.

I was sitting on the floor of my massive shower with my legs and head folded toward my chest, crying.

"What are you looking at?" Dev asked as he set a pomegranate vodka in front of me.

I handed him my phone. A play of emotions crossed his face and slowly got angrier as he flipped through the pictures.

"Tell me now that you pressed charges against this bastard." He dropped my phone on the couch and cupped my face in his hands. "Why didn't you come to me? Why didn't you let me know?"

"This happened the day you said that being with me would ruin your career. That I'd become a joke in the legal world. I couldn't turn to you. You couldn't even look at me when I left our condo."

Dev grimaced and then leaned his head against mine.

"I'm sorry, baby. I'm so sorry. I've been a complete asshole to you."

I released a deep breath and shook the sadness from me.

I was letting the stupid reporter win. This was only the first of many times someone would try to hurt me with my political ambitions.

"Dev, you can't take responsibility for this. It was Spencer Miller's fault. He broke into our house through the patio door."

"That explains why you had all the locks changed to the code system."

I nodded.

Then I detailed all that happened: Spencer's arrest, his release, and the aftermath.

"Who posted his bail?" Dev asked as he sat with me on the couch.

I brought my knees into the sofa, angling toward him. "Senator Grey Decker. Or someone who happened to be on his staff."

"That makes no sense. How did he find out about us?"

"Seriously?" I looked at Dev and sighed. "We've never truly hidden our relationship. If someone looked, they'd find the paper trail, our marriage certificate, the deed to the house that has our family trust as the owner, as well as our joint bank accounts. What we need to think about is how long he has known and why he hasn't outed us."

"He's wants to spring the information when it could hurt both Dad's and Jacinta's reputations the most. That man is dirty. If you only knew what they say about him behind closed doors."

I knew. Jacinta knew. Five years ago, when her father was up for reelection to the US Senate and her twin brother, Tyler, was running for the US House of Representatives, Grey Decker's son cornered Jacinta during a charity weekend at Decker's family estate in North Texas.

Thankfully, she'd fought him off, using the self-defense moves she'd learned in a class we'd taken during law school.

When Decker Senior heard about what had happened, he threatened to make it seem as if Jacinta was drunk and came on to his son. He even had photos doctored to make Jacinta look half-dressed and wasted.

At the time, I'd done everything in my power to get Jacinta to press charges and fight back. She'd refused, stating it could cost her family the election, especially since they'd paint her as a whore.

Through research, I'd learned Decker had used the same tactic with every woman who got in his way. He had done a great job of projecting an image of the righteous conservative politician, but those who encountered him had different opinions.

He'd hurt Jacinta in a way that made me wish horrible things on him. And because I loved my best friend, I had kept her assault by Decker's son a secret and helped her through the trauma.

Now, I had to keep her secret close to my chest, even from her brother.

"And the best way to embarrass your father and Jacinta is by throwing you and me into the spotlight. Decker is still pissed that his colleagues chose your father over him as the Senate Majority Leader. He feels slighted by the party because of his son's drug arrest, and he thinks your father swayed the vote in his favor."

"Damn, I think he's planning to do something with those pictures to hurt Dad's and Jacinta's reputations. I'm going to have to talk to Dad about this. And for the record, no matter what Dad wants me to do, I'm not hiding us anymore. I was an idiot to do that to you in the first place."

I still wasn't sure how to respond to this change in our relationship.

"You don't believe I'm sincere." A flash of hurt appeared on his face.

"We'll see once you have to deal with the press as part of your daily life."

"I've dealt with the press from the time I was born. My father is a third-generation politician."

"This is different, and you know it."

"I know, Sami. I won't let you down."

I searched his eyes, seeing the determination in them.

"I want to believe you."

"Our future is together."

I'd always believed this. Well, I had, up until I took the Bassett case.

"I hope you still feel the same after you get a true taste of the world I live in now."

He gave me a tight smile and stood, offering me his hand. "Come with me?"

I slid my fingers across his and rose from my spot on the couch.

"Where are you taking me?"

"I'm going to tuck you into bed. We'll discuss our future in the morning."

CHAPTER SEVEN

I woke with a start before I relaxed into my covers. It had been so long since I'd slept through the night without waking at least three times.

I hadn't felt this rested in months.

The moon was still out with no daylight in sight, telling me it wasn't yet six in the morning. Maybe I should go to the gym and get in a little cardio on the spin bike.

On second thought, I was going to stay right here. It felt too good to move.

Heat surrounded me, and an ache pulsed between my legs.

It must have been some dream.

I shifted to stretch when I realized the reason for my unquenched desire.

A naked Dev with a raging hard-on slept plastered to my back. He had one hand tucked down the front of my underwear, holding me tight against him.

My pulse jumped and my pussy spasmed.

I stilled and waited to see if he was awake.

His breathing was heavy, and his body was motionless.

The man always found a way to cop a feel even in his sleep.

How had we gotten in this spot?

I remembered coming upstairs with Dev and then spending the next hour just talking with him as I showered and got ready for bed.

It was exactly how it was when we'd first gotten together. Dev sat in the doorway of the bathroom and chatted with me about everything and anything he could think of while giving me the privacy I needed. The one subject we avoided was our marriage.

He never made a move on me when I'd come out wearing my sleep tank and underwear and completely surprised me when he'd tucked me into bed, kissed my forehead, and turned off the lights.

The package that was pushing against me right now was another surprise. We'd always slept naked, and I hoped since I'd put on some clothes, Devin would do the same.

I was wrong.

Devin wasn't changing the way we'd done things, even with my no-sex directive.

At the moment, I wished I'd never made the decision.

Dev's fingers rested dangerously close to my soaked slit, and all I wanted to do was shift my body and have him finish what he'd started in the car.

His breathing changed, and I turned my head to look at him. Sleepy sky-blue eyes gazed at me.

He didn't say a word but slipped his fingers between my pussy lips and started strumming my clit.

I arched up and grabbed his arm.

"Dev," I gasped.

My core throbbed and pulsed.

He rubbed and played with my sensitive flesh until I was dripping and to the point of mindless release.

Just when I couldn't take anymore, he plunged two fingers into me and ordered, "Come for me."

I cried out as my orgasm flooded through my system. My pussy contracted around Devin's digits with wave after wave of spasms.

It took so little for this man to make my body sing. He read my needs better than I did.

Hell, he was the one who'd taught me everything that I knew.

As my body slowly came down, Devin pulled out of me, licked his fingers, and shifted me to face him.

"I'm not done."

He yanked my tank top down, exposing my breasts, and then closed his lips over my nipple. He ripped my thong and plunged back into my pussy, making my body bow from the pleasurable assault.

I was mindless with need, but I had to have more. It was never one-sided with us.

I reached between our bodies, wrapped my fingers around his hard, weeping cock, and squeezed.

A moan escaped his lips as a smile touched mine.

I stroked up from the base and back down from the tip, smearing the pre-cum dripping from him.

Dev lifted his head and watched me move my hand with the grip and pace he enjoyed.

He matched my rhythm, pumping in and out of me.

He threaded his other hand through my hair, tugging my head back and locking our eyes.

Goosebumps prickled my skin, and my breath came out in pants.

God, he was the sexiest man I'd ever encountered. I traced his lower lip with my thumb and then quickly gripped one shoulder as my core quickened and a sob of burning desire erupted.

Sweat beaded his forehead and a vein pulsed on the side of his neck. The telltale sign he was close to coming.

I wished things were simpler.

I wanted to pull him toward me, to cover his lips with mine, to tell him I loved him and couldn't live without him. But I couldn't do it. He already held a part of me that I'd never get back.

We watched each other as I worked his hard rod.

All of the sudden, heat and ecstasy cascaded in my body, and another orgasm washed over me, making me grip Dev's cock tight and sending him over the edge.

"Samina, my love," he called out as my pussy continued to spasm.

Ropes of hot, sticky cum shot all over my naked breasts and tank.

I pumped him a few more times, drawing out his release until we both collapsed onto the bed, panting and heaving.

"That was..." Dev gasped.

"Intense," I responded and released a deep sigh. "I know."

Dev reached up, tugging my tank off and using it to clean my chest and body. When he finished, he threw the shirt on the floor and then opened his arms.

Without thought, I crawled to him and curled against his side. He wrapped himself around me and tucked my head under his.

"We can't give up, Sami."

"I know." A tear slipped down my cheek. "I don't want to, Dev. I'm just not sure if you'll stay once you see I'm not the same girl you fell in love with."

I closed my eyes and let exhaustion take over.

***

By the time I woke again, Dev was no longer next to me. The sheets on his side of the bed were cool to the touch, telling me he'd been up for a while.

Slowly I rolled off the mattress and headed for the bathroom. I stared at my reflection in the mirror above the sink.

My nipples had red beard marks from his ministrations, as well as small remnants of his cum dried in between my breasts.

A slow pulsing hummed in my pussy.

What was I doing with Dev? Why couldn't I keep my hands off him?

Because he's turned you into a nymphomaniac who only craves his cock.

I shook the thought from my head as the aroma of freshly brewed coffee hit my senses.

Time to get moving.

I quickly showered and dressed in a light summer maxi dress before heading to the kitchen.

As I passed through the archway, I noticed Dev scanning a group of documents on the counter with a frown on his face. He always had that look when he was trying to solve some puzzle.

He wore a fitted T-shirt and loose cotton pants, a strikingly relaxed contrast to his always put-together look. When he dressed like this, every contour of his body was visible.

The very body I shouldn't have played with earlier.

There was no way I was going to be able to resist him. I'd just have to set the boundaries before anything happened.

Who was I kidding? I was fucked.

I had to tell him before we went any further. Then I'd know if there was a solid chance to fix our relationship.

"What are you looking at?"

He lifted his gaze and gave me his "better start talking now" glare that usually scared anyone he had on the stand. Too bad it didn't have any effect on me.

"Were you going to tell me?"

"Tell you what?"

"And why is Representative Jones calling you?"

I walked up behind him, noticing the phone with five missed calls and the Senate candidacy papers I'd forgotten to put away, and cringed.

"This isn't how I wanted to tell you. For the record, I haven't filed anything with the Secretary of the Senate. And it wasn't until after Jacinta's last visit that I decided to officially throw my hat into the ring and challenge Sanders."

"So, what you're telling me is that my sister knew you were considering a bid for US Senate and I didn't."

I cocked a hand on my hip. "First of all, we've barely been in the same room for the last few months, much less had time to discuss my plans for the future. And second, Jaci is my best friend."

"I'm your husband." He towered over me. "What about Tracy Jones?"

"She's my adviser. She has experience with situations like mine."

Tracy used the notoriety she'd gained after she represented a well-known movie star in a murder trial to run for the US House of Representatives. She'd become famous more for her looks and attitude than the case itself. She was the perfect person to navigate me through the waters I was about to enter.

"Don't make Jacinta's or Mrs. Jones's political aspirations yours."

"Listen up, buster." I poked a finger into his chest. "You do not get to tell me what I do with my career. Did you consult me when you put your hat into the ring for the judgeship? You made a unilateral decision that kept me in the shadows."

"I'll admit it was one of my stupider decisions. But this is different. You're about to jump in with the big dogs. You're too nice. They'll eat you alive."

"Have you seen the people I represent? Most of them are politicians. I've handled the worst of them. Give me some credit." I fixed him with an annoyed glare. "Men have such double standards."

"Sami."

"Don't Sami me. I haven't even had a cup of coffee yet, and you're on my ass."

I pushed past Dev and grabbed the French press, pouring myself a giant mug of coffee.

After adding the perfect amount of sugar and milk, I brought the cup to my lips and chugged.

Yes, finally my morning sustenance. The bittersweet concoction ignited my cylinders and prepared me for the man growling at me.

I set the empty coffee cup on the counter.

"Now that I can function, I'll listen to your tantrum about my potential bid for US Senate."

"If you run, is the ticket going to say Kumar or Camden?"

I turned with a frown. "Of all the things to worry about, you're concerned about my name."

"Answer the question."

I lifted my chin. "Aren't there enough Senator Camdens in the world? Hell, Jacinta is positioning herself to run in Texas."

He stepped in front of me and pressed me back against the quartz island with the front of his hard, sculpted body.

The contact made my nipples harden, and there was no way to hide my reaction since I wasn't wearing a bra with the stupid dress I'd put on.

"What I want to know is are you running as the married Mrs. Camden or the single, celebrity attorney Ms. Kumar?"

His erection molded itself into my stomach and all I could do was lick my lips.

"I want to know if I'm going to be a senator's husband or in the shadows."

I scowled as my arousal cooled. "Like you did to me?"

"Yes, like the asshole I was and did to you."

"I never wanted to hide, if you recall."

"Why did you do it? Why did you accept that?"

I'd asked myself that over and over for the past five years. I'd become the cliché woman who had everything going for her and let a man take over her future.

"Because I was a stupid idiot and was desperately in love." I shifted to move away from him so he wouldn't see the lingering pain I felt, but he held me captive against the counter.

"Do you still love me or did it die over the years?"

"I never stopped loving you. I just couldn't live with things the way they were."

"Well, let's change them."

"It isn't that simple."

"Sure, it is. I'm not going anywhere, Sami."

I tilted my head up to tell him my doubts, but before I could respond, Dev's mouth covered mine and anything other than filling my physical needs became a low priority.

The kiss was the way it always was between us, all-consuming and filled with desperate desire. His tongue pushed past my lips and began a dance that made me think of how it felt to have his mouth between my legs.

I craved him as a woman starved.

Threading my fingers through his hair, I pulled him closer to me.

We tasted and savored, trying to sate our need on each other's lips.

I broke our embrace to grab the bottom of his shirt and pull it over his head.

I nearly swallowed my tongue as I took in his beautiful sculpted abs. Grazing my fingers up his stomach and gliding them to his shoulders, I yanked him back to me.

"Dev. I need you. It's been so long."

A sly smile touched his face, and then he covered my lips again, but this time the kiss was possessive as if he was claiming me, consuming me.

"You're mine, Sami," he said against my lips. "I won't let you go. I can't. You own my soul. I'll do anything to prove you come first."

My heart skipped a beat. Devin had never said that to me before. He was always a bit possessive, but he never acknowledged my claim on him.

Dev cupped my breasts through my dress, pinching the hard tips as he continued to devour my mouth.

"More," I gasped. "I want more. Please, Dev. I need you to fuck me now."

"Your wish is my command."

He lifted me onto the counter, bunching my dress around my hips.

I slid my hand between us, pushing his lounge pants down his legs and freeing his beautiful cock.

Dev brought my ass to the edge of the stone and then ripped away my thong, plunging balls-deep into my sopping pussy in a matter of seconds.

We both cried out at the exquisite feel of each other.

He grabbed my hands and placed them on the edge of the stone. "Hold on tight. I don't want you to fall, and I plan to fuck you so hard that my dick imprints itself inside your pussy."

He set a relentless pace, and all I could do was enjoy the ride. He was as desperate as I was for release.

What happened earlier was nothing compared to what was building now.

Dev pounded into me, gripping my thighs and pulling me off the counter with only my arms for leverage.

My body shook as my pussy clenched around his cock. "Dev, I can't hold out anymore. Harder, please."

He fisted my hair and yanked my head back. "Come for me, baby."

"Dev," I screamed, losing my hold on the counter as my orgasm took over.

Dev pulled me close to him, not relenting in his pace.

My mind was a wash of sensations, while my core contracted and spasmed.

Moments later, Dev followed, shouting my name and collapsing with me against the counter.

/ CHAPTER EIGHT /

I held on to Devin, letting my breath calm. We had this need that only the other could assuage.

Damn, we shouldn't have done this. It was only going to confuse our situation. How was Devin going to understand how important it was for him to support me if I gave in and fucked him every time he was in the vicinity?

I ran a hand over my face.

"Don't."

I lifted my head. "What?"

"Don't turn this into something wrong. We're married. We love each other. Making love is part of it."

Devin stood, kicking his pants the rest of the way off and holding my legs around him. He carried me to the sofa in the living room and sat with me straddling his thighs. His cock still pulsed inside me and from the feel of it, there was little chance of it going down soon.

"Our sex life has never been the problem. We use it to mask our issues."

I attempted to slip off him, but he held me tight.

"What do you need from me to prove I'm willing to change?"

"I need to know that your career doesn't come before me. I need to feel like I'm your wife in and outside of the bedroom."

"I can do that."

"Dev." I gazed into his piercing blue eyes. "I'm not kidding about running."

"I know, but as you said, you haven't announced anything yet."

I shook my head. I was only waiting for the most opportune time to make it official.

Before I could clear up his misconception, he said, "There is something I want in return."

I tried to focus on his words, but his growing erection was making me lose my train of thought. "This isn't a negotiation."

He gripped my thighs and ground his cock into me. My breath quickened and my pussy flooded around him.

"This is something we talked about years ago. Something I know you want as much as I do."

Dev lifted me and then slid me down. I gripped the back of the couch as my body ignited once again.

Then it hit me. He couldn't be talking about what he asked for yesterday.

"No," I said.

"Hear me out before you make a final decision." He tugged me up, biting the tips of my breasts.

"No. Not happening," I stuttered out as my pussy swelled and his lips moved to the other hardened nipple. "Fuck, this is not the time for this discussion. I can't think when you're distracting me."

"Then it's the perfect time to say this. I want a baby. I want you to stop taking birth control. I want a family."

I rose and glided down his length again, ignoring his words.

He couldn't be serious. When I'd brought up having a baby a year into our marriage, he'd shot the idea down. He insisted he wanted time with us as a couple first. Later, I figured out it had more to do with his family and his career. After mentioning it a few more times over the years, I gave up any hope.

A small part of me wanted to be spiteful and refuse. I'd waited so long, and Dev wanted a child now when it was convenient for him. But a more significant part of me wished for a baby.

God, how was I going to make any rational decision while riding his cock? All I could think about was him fucking me.

"We'll discuss it later and focus on this now." Dev thrust hard into me, forcing me up, and then he clutched my thighs to pull me down as he ground his girth into my cum-filled, sopping core. "Let me fuck you and then lie to me and tell me that you do not want what I want."

"Dammit, Dev, you make absolutely no sense. How the hell did you become a judge?"

He fisted my hair and yanked my head toward him, sealing our lips and making me forget everything but his throbbing cock.

He flipped me onto my back and began pounding into my quivering pussy. The ache inside me blazed into an uncontrollable euphoria. I clenched Dev's shoulders and arched against him.

"Dev," I called out. "Please."

He grinned down at me. "Come now, baby."

I detonated, squeezing and contracting around his pummeling cock. My mind clouded, and all I could see was this man who was never going to let me go.

LATER THAT AFTERNOON, I WALKED OUT TOWARD THE edge of the patio and stared at the Sound below. The view was beautiful. The blue-green water glowed against the sapphire of the sky.

Today was one of the rare true summer days where there wasn't a cloud in sight, and the temperature was a balmy eighty-five degrees.

I shouldn't have slept with him. And twice in a row. What was I thinking? I wasn't thinking, that was my problem. Whenever he was near, I was a crazed horny teenager.

This new situation with Dev gave me hope but also made me fear it would all end in disaster.

I had been planning to go ahead with the annulment that Dev said our parents had hoped would happen and begin a new life and senatorial campaign as a single woman.

When Jacinta visited, we'd discussed my options for both my personal and political future. The girl loved her brother, but she understood the pain he was causing me. I'd thought she was joking when she suggested kicking her brother to the curb and taking him for everything he had until I realized she was dead serious.

After she finished giving me her opinion on Devin, she pitched a campaign focused on the combination of my fiscally conservative and socially liberal views. Something Jacinta insisted the state of Washington and our nation needed desperately.

If only Jacinta had known that Representative Tracy Jones's daily calls had all but convinced me to take on the incumbent, Anthony Sanders, a condescending little man who had tiny dick syndrome and viewed women as disposable. Jacinta only helped solidify my decision.

I shook all thoughts of campaigning and elections from my mind as I refocused on the man who was showering in the house behind me.

I wasn't stupid enough to think sex wouldn't happen again between us, even if it was better that we restrain ourselves.

However, I couldn't live my life the way we'd done for the past five years.

He promised things would change, but I couldn't help being apprehensive. It would be so easy to fall into the fairy tale I'd thought I had before reality had shown me otherwise.

Could I trust him?

Would he pretend that we didn't exist to further his career, again? Would he cave under the pressure his father would inevitably put on him?

I closed my eyes and inhaled the salty air.

On top of everything, I was about to get on a plane and return to the heart of Texas, a place I'd left behind.

Would Papa come to see me when I was so close to Houston? At least Ashur was going to be there. I could always depend on my big brother to support me.

Hopefully, he'd convince Papa to let him bring Mummy to see me. I missed her so much. We spoke on the phone every few days, but there was nothing like spending time with her.

When I'd picked Devin over Papa, my mom had become collateral damage. Papa understood the best way to hurt me was to keep her from me. He'd hoped I'd grow to resent Dev for separating me from Mummy, but it only solidified what a manipulative bastard Papa was.

No amount of money was worth being controlled for the rest of my life.

"Stop worrying. We'll figure this out."

I turned to face Dev. "We shouldn't have slept together."

He gazed at me and then pressed me against the railing.

"Yes, we should have, and expect it to happen again and again. That's the privilege of being married. We can fuck like rabbits, and no one can say anything."

"You're incorrigible. No wonder the duped residents of Washington State love having you on the bench. Your Southern charm bamboozled them."

"If only my cloak-and-dagger skills worked on you."

He had no clue how well they did. Otherwise, I wouldn't have let myself fall into the situation I'd lived in for the past twelve years.

"Give me your left hand."

I lifted a brow and placed my palm over his. The next thing I knew, Dev was sliding my wedding band and engagement ring on my finger. A tingle shot up my spine, making my heart skip a beat.

I could never get over how beautiful the rings were. A pink diamond halo surrounded a princess-cut solitaire in an exquisite platinum setting with a matching diamond band.

I hadn't worn my rings in years, something I'd resented for the longest time.

"I want the world to know who you belong to."

"For a man who wouldn't acknowledge me in public, you're a bit possessive aren't you?"

"The Neanderthal I've kept a tight rein on for the past

few years is coming out in full force. I plan on making up for lost time. There won't be a single event either of us will attend again without the other. Everyone will know we are a couple."

"Dev, don't go crazy on my account."

"Sami, I'm serious about us. I don't ever want you to doubt how I feel about you or that you're a priority."

"What if I said I'm filing the paperwork tomorrow, and I'll be an official candidate by the time we land in Texas?" I gazed into his sapphire eyes.

"I'd support your decision and stand by you."

"I'm not sure I believe you."

"I won't lie. Elections are ruthless. The last thing I want is my wife dragged through the mud by her political opponent. However, I'll be there with you, no matter what you face. Hell, I'm an expert in campaigns and elections. Dad's run for some form of office or the other since before I was born."

I ran a thumb over his bottom lip, peering at his face.

The determined look he'd get when he meant what he said was etched all over his face.

I had to give him a chance.

The true test would come when we were in the midst of his family's Southern political world.

"Trust me, baby."

"I'll do my best." I leaned up on tiptoes and kissed him. "Come on. We have some work to do before our flight tomorrow."

CHAPTER NINE

I arrived at Austin-Bergstrom International Airport a little after one the following day. The fight was uneventful except having to get up at the ass crack of dawn and fly alone. I'd asked Ashur to send his jet to pick me up, since the last thing I wanted to deal with was fans at the airport.

Dev had taken the commercial flight out the night before to meet his parents in Houston. The good senator wanted him to meet up with a potential donor who Dev had clerked with after law school and who had very deep pockets.

I wasn't happy about him ditching me. To tell the truth, I was livid.

I should have been used to it by now, but with everything he'd said to me, I never expected for him to arrive in Austin without me.

If this was an example of putting me first, then he'd failed miserably.

A lump formed in the pit of my stomach. Was I trying to hold on to something that had no hope of a future? Or was I being unfair to Devin?

He tried to spin it as a way to make connections that could potentially help with my bid for Senate.

Devin seemed to have forgotten that my current net worth was ten times his whole family's put together, and that was *after* my father disowned me and took me out of the line to inherit his fortune. I could run my entire campaign without a cent from donors.

I had a trust that came to me free and clear when I'd turned twenty-five. It was created by my maternal grandparents who were steel industrialists in India and then used their money to become angel investors in unknown startups that netted them huge profits. No matter how much my father wished it, he couldn't revoke it.

Just because I hadn't touched a penny of it, didn't mean I wouldn't.

Who was I kidding? I was never going to dig into the trust.

I wanted to prove to myself I could succeed without using my family's money, even if my grandparents had given it to me without strings. I could proudly say I'd accomplished my goals so far. My portion of the Bassett case alone had paid for half of the build cost of my house.

Too bad Papa couldn't see past the betrayal he felt at my picking my own path in life.

What was it going to take for him to see that I wasn't a fuck-up? Any father, except mine, would be proud of everything I'd achieved.

I closed my eyes for a quick second and released a deep breath. *Let it go, Samina. You've had six years to get over Papa's actions.*

I smirked to myself. I could almost hear Jacinta singing "Let it Go," the song every parent with little girls had heard on repeat at least twenty times. She'd belt out the song off key to annoy me, in spite of the fact she had a beautiful voice.

"Mrs. Camden. Give us a few minutes to clear security, and we can exit the aircraft. Ms. Camden is waiting for you."

"Thanks, Renita. By the way, my brother put you up to calling me Mrs. Camden, didn't he?"

She blushed. "Yes, ma'am. Mr. Kumar gave me a message to relay if you asked that very question."

I waited for her to continue.

"He said it was time to face who you are, no matter what others may feel, even you."

Oh, Ash. He always knew what to say to me.

After a few minutes, the captain gave the all-clear, and I stepped down the stairs leading to the tarmac.

Before I descended halfway, Jacinta jumped out of the waiting limo and ran toward me.

I hurried the last few steps and hugged her tight.

"I missed you," I whispered as tears filled my eyes. "Things are such a mess."

"So, did you and my brother fight again or was he being his usual cheery self when he arrived this morning?"

"I haven't seen Dev since yesterday. He was meeting your parents in Houston." I furrowed my brow. "Why?"

She studied my face for a second, and then said, "Well, that answered my question. Just a warning, Big Brother is in a piss-poor mood."

"Not my problem. He left me to come here by myself when he promised to do things differently."

Jacinta hooked her arm in mine. "Come on. It looks like I have two Grumpy Gusses to deal with."

"You know you love me, no matter my mood."

"True, true. That's why I brought you a surprise."

"Oh really."

"He's been dying to see you again."

I stopped midstep and placed a hand on my hip. "Who's he?"

"Me," a raspy voice answered.

Excitement filled me, and I rushed past Jacinta and toward the car, where my sexy-as-sin and gorgeous childhood friend, Veer George, stood. It had been months since I'd seen him, and I hadn't realized how much I missed my adopted brother until he stepped out of the limo.

"Veer, I missed you so much."

He grabbed me by the waist, spinning me around.

"How are you, shorty? Has your husband come to his senses or am I going to have to steal you from him?"

He set me back on the ground and gestured for us to enter the open door.

I climbed in and moved to the opposite end of the seats.

"You may just have to. On second thought, I don't need any more things added to my plate."

"I agree. Let's not poke the angry bear. You know how Dev gets when it comes to Sam." Jacinta grinned as she scooted in next to me. "The last thing you need after announcing your bid for the governorship is a fist fight with a federal judge who happens to be a senator's son."

"I think I'll have the constituents' support when they learn I was defending the honor of my childhood friend, who I consider a sister."

"Speaking of, I have a question I've meant to ask you." I took a sip of the water that Jacinta handed me.

"Shoot."

"When did you decide to become a politician? I thought you hated the drama of politics?"

"Jacinta convinced me that my views would be a refreshing change to the status quo we've had in Texas for decades."

I lifted a brow in Jacinta's direction. "You do realize he'll be running against the governor who represents your political party?"

"Just because I'm a conservative doesn't mean I

wouldn't vote for an independent if he or she was the right candidate."

"I'd be an underdog going against the establishment," Veer said, "but I think even conservatives will come on board when they hear my stance on key issues important to the state."

I saw a look pass between Jacinta and Veer that made me think I was missing something.

Veer continued, "It also helps that our current governor has higher political aspirations which makes him look like he is only using his position as a placeholder."

"Care to inform me when I stepped into the Twilight Zone of politics? First, you're pushing me to run in Washington, and now you've convinced Veer to run. Jacinta Ellen Camden, why are you on this crusade to get all your friends into politics?"

A look passed in her eye and I wished I hadn't asked the question. I knew the answer. Jacinta hadn't planned to make her first political run a bid for US Senate, but the moment Decker covered up his son's assault on her, she'd made it her life's mission to make sure no Decker would ever hold any office again, especially Decker Senior.

"Let's just say, I've encountered too many old-boys'-club types living here in Austin." Her mouth tightened for a moment. "And I think it's time for some new blood. You and Veer represent something different."

"Yeah, we're both Indian." I played along so that Veer wouldn't pick up on the tension underlying Jacinta's words.

"Sam, I'm not talking about your race, and you know it. It's your stance on economics, social issues, and leadership."

"Are you aware my running does not affect Texas politics? I'm a resident of the state of Washington now."

I'd made the decision to stay in Seattle a few days after moving into the house. I had a successful career, and whether Devin was in my life or not had no bearing. Yes, I missed my friends and my old life in Texas, but it had been years, and things would never be the same.

"We aren't the only ones she's on a mission to get elected." Veer shook his head. "She's called half of your old study group from Stanford and every non- overly left-wing or right-wing friend to get involved in the election system."

"If all goes according to plan—" a calculating gleam hit Jacinta's eyes, "—the three of us, plus at least twenty-five others I know, will go head-to-head against incumbents who represent the bureaucracy our nation is tired of dealing with every day. We will be a group of leaders who take into account not only our parents' generation but also those who are children right now. We are the bipartisan wave of the future."

The girl had her pitch down pat. "Jaci, how long did you practice that speech in front of the mirror?"

"About an hour. How did I do?" She grinned at me.

"You could work on your enthusiasm a bit."

"I'll be sure to do better next time."

"The both of you are mental. I almost feel sorry for

Devin when you two get together." Veer took a sip of his drink while shaking his head.

"When did you and my brother become buddies?" Jacinta crossed her arms in front of her and cocked a brow.

I wondered the same thing. Veer and Dev barely said two words to each other whenever our friends circle gathered. They tended to speak to everyone else but each other.

"We aren't. I said, I almost feel sorry for him. Until Devin Camden does right by her, the only side I'm on is Samina's."

"When have you been on anyone else's side?" Jacinta grumbled, making me think I was missing something. "You take the almost-big-brother thing to a whole new level."

"When Ashur and I deployed overseas, I made a promise to always watch out for Samina, whether Ash was around or not. It was a vow Ash never had to ask me to make. I'm an only child, and Ash and Sam are the closest I'll ever get to having siblings. They are my family. I'll do whatever I can to protect them."

"We love you too, V." I reached over and clasped Veer's hand in mine. "I'm so thankful both my brothers came home. Although a little banged up."

I remembered how scared I was when I'd heard Ash and V were injured during a firefight in South Sudan where their planes had gone down. The three of us would do a weekly video chat to keep me up to date, but for weeks I'd heard nothing from either of them. And then my father had gotten a call informing us that both Ash and V had suffered brain injuries and were in comas. It was one of the worst times of my life.

The Air Force had transferred them to a military hospital in Germany and then returned them home once they woke and were stable enough to endure an overseas flight.

"You and me both." He squeezed my fingers as he rubbed the scar that ran from his right temple down to his jaw with his other hand.

Before the accident, Veer had been handsome in the Bollywood dark, brooding, and sexy way, but the scars had given him an added bad-boy appeal. Ash would say V now had a pirate look that made panties drop.

I needed to set him up with one of my girls from back home. He was a total catch and deserved someone who loved him and saw past his money and his always-controlled demeanor.

"Hey, I have a fabulous idea," Jacinta said, snapping me out of my matchmaking thoughts.

Veer and I looked at each other and winced. Jacinta's ideas had a way of putting me in situations I regretted later.

Our parents should have thought better than to put two overly sheltered eighteen-year-old child prodigies together. I still remembered when Papa told me the only way I'd attend Stanford was if I lived with Jacinta, whose father was a conservative politician from Louisiana. It had taken less than an hour after our parents left us in our apartment for the first adventure to start, something to do with trying to sneak into a bar, and our escapades continued for the next three years.

I still remembered the hell Devin, Ashur, and Veer gave me when they had to fly to California to keep Jacinta and me from getting expelled for public streaking. It started off as a fun celebration of our mutual twenty-first birthdays that fell close together. Then it turned into too many shots and a game of truth-or-dare with our much-older classmates. Thankfully, the three men were able to keep any news of the incident under wraps, and our parents never heard a peep about it.

"Okay, let's hear it. And for the record, I am not announcing my candidacy yet. Veer can be your one conquest on your election endeavors for this weekend."

I wanted a few more weeks to solidify my strategy before it became public knowledge.

"Even though that would be a wonderful addition to this weekend, my plan involves something a bit more fun. Well, for me anyway. It will also solve many of your problems."

This should be good.

"Spit it out, Jacinta."

"I want Devin to think Veer is replacing him."

CHAPTER TEN

"No. Absolutely not," Veer challenged Jacinta. "I am not going to be used to make Devin jealous."

"Oh, come on." Jacinta crossed her arms. "It's a fabulous idea. It was Sam who put the idea in my head."

"No. He already sees red every time I'm anywhere near you, his baby sister. How do you think he'll react if you fuck with him when it comes to Sam?"

I frowned. "Care to explain that comment?"

"Sam, he thinks I'm competition for your affections." He stared at me as if I'd asked a stupid question.

"Wait. What? I though your mutual dislike had to do with my secret marriage and not being public with our relationship."

"Well, you thought wrong," Jacinta interjected. "When I told Dev the list of people who were joining us on the riverboat and came to Veer's name, he growled. The always-poised, never-reveal-his-true-feelings Judge Devin James Camden growled. I loved it."

"You can't be serious. That's just gross." I scrunched up my nose. "I think I just threw up a little in my mouth. V, you're hot and all, but no."

"Feeling's mutual." He glared at Jacinta, who tried to ignore him.

I was not going to be a party to this. My life was complicated enough.

"Aren't you the one who said not to poke the angry bear? Dev and I are trying to fix our marriage, not destroy it with no hope of repair."

"My plan will work in your favor."

"How?"

"Veer is your dad's version of a wet-dream son-in-law. He is the son of a business partner, well educated, a war hero, and most importantly, shares your cultural background."

"No!" I shouted as a tinge of anger flared to life. "And that's final. I'm fighting all the people who've tried to control me my entire life and now you want me to do something to manipulate Dev. I can't believe you would suggest something like this."

Her eyes grew big, telling me she realized she'd crossed a line.

"Sorry, Sam. Forget it. I just want Dev to see that he could lose you if he doesn't change the way things are going. I love the both of you so much. You're my family and I want it to remain that way."

My irritation evaporated. "I know, Jaci, but you have to let Dev and me fix the mess we created." A line formed between her brows and she opened her mouth to argue, but I spoke again. "I'm as much at fault as he is, no matter what either of you believe. I've thought about it. I accepted this fucked-up marriage because I love him more than anyone ever could and because..." I trailed off.

Was I ready to admit something I hadn't verbalized but knew was true?

"And because?" Jacinta probed.

I looked out the window and noticed the group of reporters and "Hot Stuff" fans waiting outside of the driveway leading to Jacinta's house.

"Saved from answering the question we all know the answer to by the relentless media," Jacinta muttered.

I covered my face with my hands. "They followed me here from Seattle? Why won't they leave me alone?"

Another look passed between Veer and Jacinta.

"Want to tell her, or should I?" Jacinta asked.

"Tell me what?"

"You do the honors. She's your best friend."

"If you two are done talking about me, I'd appreciate an answer to my question."

"Sam, your secret is out. The Bassett Hound announced you were already married and he couldn't set you up anymore."

"And?" It was like pulling teeth to get a straight answer.

"And now he's decided that you would make the

perfect candidate for president. He is on a mission to convince you to run."

"What?" I exclaimed and looked out the window again.

Sign after sign had "Kumar for President."

Well, hell, why didn't I skip the senatorial election and jump right into becoming a presidential candidate?

"Stop looking at me like that, Jacinta Ellen Camden. The presidential election isn't for two and a half more years. Outside of being born in the United States, I'm not qualified. I'm neither old enough nor have the experience."

"Well, that didn't stop our current president. I'm not talking about his age, by the way," Veer interjected, resulting in a glare from Jacinta. "What? He's a real-estate tycoon with no political knowledge prior to running for office. At least Sam knows the law."

I shook my head. "This is not the time for a debate between Mr. Liberal and Ms. Conservative."

"I'm not a liberal, I'm an independent," Veer countered.

Jacinta snorted. "Same difference."

"Hey, I take offense to that. I'm an independent, too." I gave an exaggerated scowl and wagged my finger at Jacinta. "Plus, you're the one who just went through a whole pitch to get me to run for Senate."

"Whatever. You never let me have any fun," she grumbled with a smirk on her face.

That's when I realized she had orchestrated the

conversation to keep my mind off the paparazzi until we passed through the compound's gates.

"You think you're so clever."

"You're not the only child prodigy in the car. And for the record, I wasn't referring to you, Veer," Jacinta said as the car pulled up to her house.

"God, I love this house. It's the perfect combination of Southern plantation and modern architecture." I gazed up at the two-story mansion Jacinta called home.

"If you hadn't hooked up with my brother and moved up to Seattle, we could have lived here together."

The mention of Devin made my stomach fill with anxiety and desire.

Just like Clint had said, that man had me twisted inside and not knowing what I wanted.

"Speaking of Devin. Where is he?" I tried to keep the hope I felt from my voice but failed miserably.

Jacinta lifted a brow and then answered, "He was in some meetings with Dad. Something about planning out his future. Oh, to be a fly on that wall, when Dev handed Dad his ass. One day my father will realize he has no say in what his children decide to do with their careers."

"What are you talking about?" The only thing I knew about Devin's last conversation with his father was that he'd told them about me.

"For a married couple, y'all need to talk more instead of banging each other's brains out."

"Shut up, you're such an ass."

"Takes one to know one."

"Ladies, if you're done acting like children, I suggest we table any more discussions about politics and media. There are eyes and ears everywhere. The house won't be secure as long as all the extra staff is here. Then even less so when all the guests arrive."

"Jaci, how many people did you invite? I know you are trying to hobnob with the political elite but you usually keep it to a minimum."

The door opened and she slipped out as she responded. "I did what was necessary." And headed toward the side door of the house.

"Well that clears up absolutely nothing." I scowled at Veer.

"Don't look at me. She's your best friend."

I stepped out of the limo and waited for Veer. "But you two have become chummy since she moved here."

"The fact we socialize on occasion because we live in the same city means nothing," he said as he watched Jacinta with a predatory twinkle in his eye.

"I don't buy that for a second. An acquaintance doesn't have the ability to convince someone to run for governor or make him look at her as if he'd like to lick every inch of her body."

"Let it go, half pint. Remember what I said about eyes and ears." He placed his hand on my waist and guided me toward the house. "I'll escort you inside and then make my way home. I have to tidy up my house before my parents arrive. You know how they get when I don't have everything in the proper place."

"Be nice. Uncle and Auntie are the sweetest people I know. I think you want to get home to hide any evidence of all those illicit affairs you like having."

"I'm a political candidate. I don't have time for a moment alone, much less a romantic liaison with anyone."

"Welcome to the world of media intrusion." I smiled up at him and winked.

I caught sight of Dev looking down at us from the second-story balcony of Jacinta's giant house. He clenched his jaw and turned back to listen to whatever his father was saying to him.

Just perfect. I wasn't here more than a minute and I'd pissed him off.

At that moment, two reporters jumped out of the bushes. One took pictures and the other shouted questions. Within seconds, Jacinta's security team tackled them.

Veer pushed me behind him.

"What will your husband say about you arriving here with Mr. George?" the man asked, even though he was cuffed and his face pushed into the ground. "Is he a family friend or more? How does your new celebrity impact your career? Is Mr. George planning to use your popularity to help his campaign?"

I ignored him, but I couldn't help but shake. Images of what had happened with Spencer Miller flashed before my eyes as well as the fear I'd felt, knowing someone had gotten so close to me.

"Come on, Sam. Let's get you inside."

We ran toward the side entrance of the house leading

into the kitchen and then I collapsed on one of the barstools surrounding the granite island.

I inhaled deep and then dropped my head onto the counter. This sucked.

Not only was I a complete wimp when it came to paparazzi, I was letting others handle my problems instead of facing them myself. A tear slipped down my cheek.

I had to get it together. I could stare down the scariest of opponents without flinching in the courtroom and now I was falling apart at every turn.

"Here. Drink this. It will take the edge off." Jacinta handed me a drink, but the second I smelled it, my stomach turned.

"I just need some sparkling water."

Within a few moments, Jacinta's housekeeper rushed over, giving me a glass of the fizzy liquid.

"God, how the fuck did they get on my land?" Jacinta pulled out her phone and began to text. "From this point on, no one will have access to any part of this property without clearance." She glanced at Veer, who nodded and left the room, and then she approached me, taking my hands in hers. "I'm so sorry this happened."

She knew how devastated I had been after the whole Spencer Miller debacle, especially when Decker used his political pull to have Miller's charges dropped to a misdemeanor instead of a felony.

At that moment, Dev rushed in.

"Baby, are you okay?" He pulled me into his arms.

I buried my head against his chest, clutching his shirt

under my fingers. He smelled of spiced cologne and soap. A scent so comforting, I could get lost in it.

And I did. A sob escaped my lips and within the next few seconds I was releasing months of worry, apprehension, and chaos.

I never cried and now I was doing it at every turn, and for some reason, having Dev hold me made the havoc and violation of the media invasion of my life even more prominent.

What I wouldn't have given for him to have held me when Miller broke into our house and made me think he'd have done more to me than take pictures if I hadn't pressed the panic button in our bathroom.

Dev picked me up, cradling me in his arms as I cried.

"Let it out, baby," he whispered into my hair. "I've got you. I'm so sorry I wasn't there for you before. I'm here now."

When the last of my weeping subsided, I looked up to find the kitchen empty, with Dev and me the only occupants.

I lifted my gaze to Dev's worried one. "Thank you."

"You've been so strong for so long. The least I could do was hold you when you needed to let go of the reins." He thumbed a stray tear.

"I don't know what's wrong with me. I should be used to this type of thing by now. Hell, if I don't have a day where a reporter doesn't jump out of nowhere to ask questions, then my day isn't complete."

"I'm beginning to really hate Clint Bassett."

"Let's be honest. Ever since I took Senator Xander's case two years ago, my name has been in the spotlight."

A former staffer had accused the senator of forcing him to cover up an affair she denied having. He had tried to blackmail her, and when she decided to press charges, I took the case. In the end, after an extensive probe into the allegations, Senator Xander was exonerated. The investigation revealed the staffer was part of a plot to ruin the senator's character because of her support and stance on women's reproductive rights.

This was the case that had put me in the national spotlight and the one that had revealed the cracks in my relationship with Devin.

"Yes, but it wasn't to this level." He inhaled deep. "I'm sure you saw the groupies outside the gates. It's only going to get worse."

"I know. Especially when I announce I'm running."

He didn't respond to my comment but said, "Come on. Let me get you upstairs. Take a nap and then we'll go meet with my parents."

I nodded, not commenting on the fact he'd ignored my statement, and slipped off his lap. He led me up a set of stairs from the back of the kitchen and to a guest room I assumed was mine.

All of my bags were inside, as well as Devin's.

"So, we're sharing a room this time? No pretending I'm only your sister's best friend."

He closed the door, walked up to me, and untucked my

shirt, pulling it over my head. "Everyone knows you're my wife and have been for almost five years."

Goosebumps prickled my skin as the cool air from the air conditioner hit my body.

He unbuttoned my jeans, pushing them over the curve of my bottom and down my thighs, and then he lowered himself to kneeling. "Lift your leg."

I followed his command, stepping out of my pants, and waited. His breath was dangerously close to my panty-covered crotch.

My insides grew hot as arousal took seed inside my core.

His breath changed, and he licked his lips as he stared at the growing dampness wetting my underwear.

"Devin," I whispered.

"No, baby, not now." He stood and pushed me toward the bed.

He lifted the covers.

A yawn escaped my lips and made me realize how tired I was from all my crying.

A nap was something I rarely indulged in, but since Dev insisted, why not?

"Get in. You're exhausted. I'll be here when you wake. I promise to satisfy you then."

"I'll hold you to it."

CHAPTER ELEVEN

"Wake up, Sami."

I roused from a deep sleep to the feel of heat and need burning my body.

My pussy was swollen and throbbed for release.

I opened my eyes and saw Dev's feet sticking out the bottom of the comforter.

His hands glided along my inner thighs, making my pulse jump, and his body weight pressed my legs into the bed.

It had been years since he'd woken me this way.

"Devin." I lifted the covers to see him crawling upward.

"Shh. I'm busy. I promised my wife that I'd satisfy her when she woke." He smiled up at me with mischief in his eyes.

He looked years younger, like the way he had when we'd first met, twelve years ago.

He butterflied my legs apart, exposing my wet center to his gaze.

His fingers traced the outside of my labia, sliding my thong between my dampening folds, and then squeezed, working my lower lips in a slow seductive rhythm designed to make me insane.

Every nerve ending woke with a vengeance, making my body arch against him.

My nipples pebbled and my breasts swelled as my clit throbbed for more.

He pulled my minuscule underwear against me, making me cry out.

"I'm almost there."

"No, you're not." He stopped his ministrations and lifted his body up, throwing the duvet off us.

I growled. "I thought this was about satisfying me?"

He pulled his shirt over his head, revealing a body sculpted to perfection from hours of training for triathlons. His beautiful cock strained against the seam of his jeans, making my mouth water for a lick.

I sat up, getting onto my knees, and ran my nails up from his waist, over his abs, and along his pecs. His skin was hot to the touch and covered in a light dusting of blondish-brown hair that tickled the tips of my fingers.

"It is, but that doesn't mean I can't enjoy seeing you squirm." He fisted my hair as our lips met, devouring each other.

His mouth tasted of cinnamon and brandy, telling me Jacinta had served some of her signature cocktails.

I grazed my palm over his fabric-covered cock, stroking up and down his length.

Just as I deepened our embrace and began to unbutton his pants, he pushed me back onto the bed, yanked my feet out from under me, and wedged his way between my legs.

"You aren't going to distract me. I'm on a mission." With a quick jerk of his hand, my thong was ripped from my body.

"Do you know how many pairs of underwear I've had to replace over the years?"

He leaned down and blew on my center. "Are you complaining?"

Goosebumps prickled my sensitized skin. I shook my head. "Absolutely not."

He pushed two fingers deep into my soaked core and covered my pulsing clitoral nub with his mouth.

"God, you taste better than ever."

His tongue circled and strummed my clit as his fingers curled inside, hitting the spot that made my pussy clench in a tight grip around him.

I was helpless as the first tide of sensation washed over me.

I threaded my hands through his hair and arched up.

"Devin," I screamed.

My pussy clenched and pulsed, flooding the pistoning fingers inside me. This man could play my body like a concert pianist.

A hand slid up my belly holding me in place, while the other strummed the G-spot inside me.

"More," he murmured against my pussy. "Give me one more."

His mouth continued its exquisite torture of licking and sucking until I shattered again in a writhing, heaving mess.

I took deep, hard breaths as I stared up at the plastered crown molding that gave away the age of the historic house.

My body felt numb and blissfully content.

Dev shifted to lie beside me, his face flushed with desire and breaths coming out in short pants.

I leaned over him, kissing his jaw. "Your turn."

He grabbed me and pulled me against his chest. "No, this was about you. I plan to fuck you until you pass out later."

I listened to the steady beat of his heart.

"I'm sorry I left you to come here without me. I wouldn't have gone unless it was absolutely necessary."

"Dev, was meeting this man so important? If I wanted to, I could finance a campaign with the money my grandparents left me."

"I know this."

"Then why?"

"Because I know you'd eat dirt before touching your inheritance. It doesn't matter that the money came from your mother's side. It represents the millions of ways your dad tried to control you and tell you that you'd never make it without it."

I had no idea what to say. Dev had verbalized something I hadn't ever expressed to him.

From the moment Papa discovered I could do complex equations as a six-year-old, he'd planned my life for me. He had pulled me out of my top-of-the-line private school and hired some of the best tutors money could buy.

He used his money and influence to control every aspect of my life, from the schools I would apply to for college to picking my major. He was the reason I'd become a lawyer.

The only decision I'd made for myself before marrying Dev was applying to Stanford for law school instead of Harvard as my father expected.

No matter how successful I was in life, if I didn't follow Papa's plan, I was a failure.

"Dev, will he ever accept me?"

He sighed and kissed the top of my head. "I wish I could say yes, but your father believes you made a fool of him when you married me and moved to Washington."

"I miss my mom. Do you think he's going to let Ashur bring her here tomorrow?"

"I don't know, baby. Ash will try, but ultimately your father makes the decisions."

"I wish Mummy would stand up to him, even though I know she never will. Papa has her under his thumb, and she's too scared to challenge him."

"Sami, your dad is a powerful man, and according to Ash, you're the only one who has ever turned your back on him, his aspirations, and his money. It pisses him off that he has no hold over you, so the only way to get back at you is to keep you from your mother."

"I just wish..."

"Sam, you have to stop hoping for his approval—it's never going to come. You don't prescribe to his plan for your life."

I lifted my head and glared down at him. "You're one to talk."

A knock on the door saved me from a grumpy response.

"Dev, if you're done waking Sam up, Dad has requested your presence for a family discussion. I suggest you and Sam hurry. Something is up and one of you is the cause of it."

I glanced at Dev, who shrugged his shoulders and slipped off the bed, pulling me with him.

"Let's get this over with."

DEV AND I ARRIVED AT JACINTA'S PRIVATE LIBRARY TEN minutes after she left us. It was one of my favorite rooms in the house. Floor-to-ceiling shelves of books and nooks and crannies filled with comfy couches made the perfect place to relax and lose oneself in the pages of a novel.

As we entered the room, I felt a distinct edge of tension.

Dev's brother Tyler, who I hadn't seen since February, paced with a worried expression on his face, Jacinta and

Carol nursed cocktails without looking in our direction, and the senator was on the phone, red-faced and reaming the person on the other line.

"Samina dear." Carol jumped up and wrapped me in a tight hug. "I'm so glad everything is out in the open now. From the time you roomed with Jaci, you were always part of this family, but now it's official and permanent."

I squeezed her back and let her warmth soak in. There was nothing like a hug from a mother who cared about you.

"I see how it is. We both come in at the same time, and all you see is Sami. I thought I was your favorite child." Dev pouted with his bottom lip sticking out.

Jacinta snorted from her place on the sofa

"Your place in the favorite hierarchy is questionable at best, Devin James Camden. It's going to take me some time to get over how you hid Samina from us. And we haven't had our conversation yet. You've spent most of yesterday and this morning doing God knows what and then the moment you arrived here you were locked up with your father."

Carol released me, guiding me to a spot between Jacinta and her on the sofa. I lifted a brow in Dev's direction, who pretended he didn't notice my unsaid question about his suspicious whereabouts.

I nodded toward Tyler, Jacinta's twin. "Good to see you, Ty. How's Charlotte?"

I had given Tyler a rescued shepherd-husky mutt when his fiancée broke up with him and took the dog they shared.

Of all the Camden siblings, he was the funniest as well as the most sensitive. He hid his true emotions behind a wall of humor and impeccable Southern charm. The only people who saw the genuine Tyler underneath was his family.

"Good, as always. I left my girl at home. She misses you."

"Then you better bring her to the house next time you visit."

"Nothing like a puppy to heal a broken heart," Jacinta said as she handed me a drink.

I brought the drink to my nose, and one whiff of it made my stomach turn.

I handed it back to her.

"Did you leave any alcohol in the bottle?" I asked. "If I drink that, I'm going to be useless, and something tells me I'm going to need all my wits for the discussion ahead."

A minute later, Dev's father ended his call.

"Samina, it's good to see you." With a forced smile, he came over to shake my hand.

"Senator."

"Call him Richard, if not Dad." Carol patted my leg and fixed the senator with an annoyed stare.

"There's something we need to discuss." He ignored his wife's words. No doubt Dev got his tactics from his father. "I heard what Decker did to you."

I turned to Devin, who leaned against the doors leading to the patio.

"You told him."

"Yes, Sami. He needed to know what was going on under his nose."

"And?" I probed, sneaking a quick look at Jacinta, who was wringing her hands together.

No one seemed to notice her agitation at the mention of Decker's name.

"I'm going to meet with some of my colleagues to handle it my way," the senator stated.

"Meaning?"

Devin answered, "Decker made an enemy when he went after you to get back at Dad."

I bet it had less to do with me and more the fact Devin was associated with an alleged scandal of a secret marriage.

"I will make his life a living hell for trying to orchestrate a scandal with one of my children. His son's arrest will be the least of his worries. I was hoping to let Jacinta run this election her way, but after this, I'm going to use every connection I have to make sure Jaci gets the party nomination."

I couldn't believe the reason he was going to openly support Jacinta's run for Senate was that Decker pissed him off. As a father, I'd expect him to be one of her biggest supporters, but I should have known better. He hadn't given Tyler an ounce of recognition when he'd run for the United States House of Representatives. He'd said he wanted Tyler to run on his own merit, but then he'd taken all the credit once Tyler won.

Jacinta was her party's darling and the up-and-coming hopeful for the highest office in the nation. Her popularity was higher than her father's, and instead of helping his daughter, he'd used her status to benefit his campaign. Richard had so many traits that reminded me of my own father, but I kept those thoughts to myself.

Jacinta adored her father. He was the reason she'd entered politics. She'd tell me he wasn't the typical conservative. I never had the heart to tell her she viewed him through rose-colored glasses.

"Spencer Miller broke into our house to make money from the pictures Decker hired him to take," I said. "Miller was planning to double-cross Decker up until his arrest. I had him investigated. A tabloid had offered him six hundred thousand."

A look passed between Dev and Richard.

"Both Dad and I agree with you," Dev said. "It was too much of a coincidence that Decker was available to help Miller. There is no way to cover up an incident like yours without long-term planning. That's way I had Tyler do some digging. Tell her what you found out."

Tyler stopping pacing and leaned against the back of a recliner in the corner of the room. "I used my contacts to trace what accounts paid for the bail. Decker has had Miller on a ten-thousand-dollar monthly stipend from before the break-in. I believe he made plans starting from the time Dad won Senate Majority Leader. Your marriage is public record. It just wasn't acknowledged. And if spun correctly, a perfect scandal."

"I've dealt with the manipulation and double-talk of

politicians and celebrities over and over again, and now I've been a pawn in one of their schemes."

Jacinta winced at my words, and I cringed inside. I was in a room full of politicians and would become one soon.

"You better get used to it. If Devin is giving up his judicial prospects for a political bid on your part, you'll have to face the fact that anything and everything about you is fair game," Richard said.

"Since when is breaking into someone's house, taking nude pictures of them, and threatening to rape them fair game?" I pinched the bridge of my nose, trying to soothe a headache that had flared to life. "If I were a man, this type of tactic would never be considered or tolerated."

Richard shrugged and then said, "It all comes with the territory."

I couldn't believe my violation was something he viewed as par for the course. And I thought *my* father was ruthless and manipulative.

I lifted my chin and stared Richard in the eyes. "My question to you is, if this were Jacinta in the same situation, would you feel the same way?"

I didn't dare glance at Jacinta. I'd see pain etched all over her face. Her father's answer would seal his fate in her eyes.

"If you can't handle it, then I suggest you learn to keep a lower profile. This is only the beginning, little girl. Let's hope you don't have any scandalous pictures other than you sitting on the floor of a shower. The media will have a field day with pictures of you with a past lover."

"Dad, watch it," both Dev and Tyler ordered at the same time.

"Don't ever speak to her like that again." Dev moved behind me, placing a hand on my shoulder. "She's my wife, and you will show her respect."

"I'm telling her the truth. Politics is ruthless," Richard challenged. "She needs to learn. She's about to enter the big leagues, and her gender doesn't mean anyone will take it easy on her. I wouldn't."

"So, what you're saying is that you'd hire someone to take compromising pictures of all your opponents, male or female, to win an election. You'd condone it as collateral damage if in the process the victim was assaulted?" My gaze bored into the senator's.

"I said no such thing. Don't you dare question my integrity, girl."

My temper hit an all-time high. This fucker was going to get it, but Carol placed a hand on my leg and squeezed.

"Richard, enough." Carol's face grew cold. "I suggest you think before you speak, or one of your sons may be the one to challenge you for your seat next election. And I will be more than happy to support them."

"You're on her side? Our son has turned his back on a possible appointment to the United States Supreme Court. He's giving up his dream for her."

"Dad, that was your dream, not mine," Devin said from behind me.

"I have never asked him to give up anything for me." I

clenched my fists. "I'm the one who's given up so much over the years for both of you."

I stood. I wasn't going to put up with shit from him, especially when I refused to do it for my own father.

"Let me make this clear to you, Senator. Your son chooses the path he walks. I've rarely been a factor in his decisions. I moved to another state for him."

"Bullshit. If it weren't for you, Devin would never have left Louisiana. Because of you, he lives halfway across the country." He laughed. "Just wait. All your father's money isn't going to protect you from what you're about to jump into. DC will eat you alive. Those pictures you allowed the reporter to take are the least of your worries."

"Richard, how dare you?" Carol shouted.

"No, Carol. It's okay. I've dealt with men like him and the games they play from the time I clerked for Judge Kerry. I've handled more than my share of male egos."

It was hard enough trying to make a name for myself in the legal field, and then add in the fact I was barely out of puberty, a female, and small in size, made me learn how to assert myself in a male-dominated field.

I clenched my fists and then felt Dev at my side. He linked his fingers with mine.

"I never thought I'd see the day that you'd blame the victim for a crime committed against them. You're the exact type of good old boy who needs replacing," Jacinta said through clenched teeth as she rose from the sofa and joined Dev and me, threading her fingers through mine on the other side. "I've never been more ashamed of you than I am right now."

Richard staggered as if Jacinta had hit him. "You don't mean that."

"Yes, Richard. She does. As do all of us. In the forty years we've been together, we've disagreed about many things, but I've never thought I didn't know you. I truly have no idea who you are." Carol stood and walked toward the door. "Ladies, I think it's time for some fresh air. Care to join me?"

CHAPTER TWELVE

"Will you answer a question for me?" Carol asked as she poured me a glass of iced tea.

I nodded. "Yes, ma'am."

After leaving the senator and his sons in the library, Carol, Jacinta, and I had decided to have a drink and snacks on the back deck of the house.

Jacinta and Carol had created a giant spread of cookies, tea sandwiches, and pastries, even laying out a white lacy cotton tablecloth on the patio table for our yummy fare.

I could tell both women were visibly shaken by what had transpired and needed something to take their minds off the argument.

I'd tried to help, but they only shooed me away, saying they had everything under control.

"Why do you want to run? Don't pretend you haven't decided. I know when someone's put their name into the arena of politics."

I had waited for someone to ask me that question and I could always trust Carol to go to the source for anything she wanted to know.

"I want to run because no one expects it of someone like me." Carol pursed her lips at my response, making me clarify what I meant. "I don't fit the mold. When it comes to spending, I'm conservative. When it comes to social issues, I'm liberal. There are a lot of incumbents who feel threatened by people like me because of my appeal to the centrists."

Especially the man I'd go up against in the election.

Senator Anthony Sanders was a person who'd dismissed me the first time we'd met at a charity fundraiser. He'd barely paid attention to anything I had to say, and I happened to be the main speaker for the evening. He'd treated me like a cute, pretty face. Then had the nerve to turn to a junior attorney in my firm to ask his opinion of the very topic I'd brought up. It wasn't until the emcee had introduced me that he'd realized his mistake in dismissing me.

That was the day I'd realized this man had to go.

"Aren't you afraid about your privacy and how everyone will react to your relationship with Devin? I know your potential opponent. He views his job as a career and he will pull every trick in the book to keep it. What Richard said is true. I'm not saying it's right, but your opponent will use your pain as a way to elevate his position. He'll shame you into hiding."

As a wife of a politician, I guessed Carol had seen and

heard more than she would ever let on. Her insight wasn't anything I hadn't learned for myself.

"I don't have a choice but to face Sanders head-on, no matter what he throws my way. The day I became a celebrity attorney was the day my privacy started walking out the door. Clint just pushed it to a level I never anticipated."

"That's an understatement," Jacinta added and lifted her glass to her lips.

"Excuse me, miss. My career path is your fault. You're the one who introduced me to Representative Jones and suggested I'd be the best attorney for her case."

"Jacinta Ellen Camden, how could you send that awful woman to her?"

"Mom, Tracy isn't that bad. She speaks her mind, and she doesn't agree with Dad's viewpoints."

If Carol only knew that Tracy Jones was the one who put the bug in my ear to run for office years ago and was now my political adviser. Poor Carol was in for a shock when she found out.

I broke the glaring contest between the mother-daughter duo and said, "I'm not worried about my relationship status. As Tyler stated, I've never hidden our relationship. I just never acknowledged it in public. If anyone investigated me, they'd find I've lived and shared a home with Devin from the beginning of our marriage."

"What about the separation? Don't you think the press will figure out you're legally separated?" Jacinta asked.

Carol dropped the cookie she was about to bite into.

"Say that again. You two aren't together anymore? But... but what about all the sex you two are obviously having? Don't try to deny it. I know exactly how Devin woke you up earlier."

I winced, glared at Jacinta, and then peeked toward the library window. Dev paced as he discussed something with his father.

Most likely me.

"I never filed anything. I had Tara draft a separation decree and send it to Devin. However, I never took the step to have it recorded with the court."

Jacinta smacked me on the shoulder. "You sneaky girl."

"Don't scare me like that, young lady." Carol fanned herself with her hand. "In my opinion, you should have kicked his ass into gear years ago. Then maybe I'd have a baby to take care of while you're on the campaign trail."

My eyes just about bugged out of my head as the tea went down the wrong pipe, making me cough. She was always the poised Southern lady, and she was throwing jabs right and left without trying to cover it up with genteel grace.

I looked at Jacinta, who seemed as surprised as I was.

"Mom, I swear, I thought you'd be on his side."

Carol cocked a hand on her hip. "He's my oldest son but that doesn't mean I won't recognize when he's wrong. Or when you are." She paused and took my hand in hers. "You allowed a man to dictate how you lived your life. What was wrong with you?"

"It's complicated. All I can say is that I've come to my

senses and decided that I had to make my needs a priority for a change, and at this time in my life, it is my career."

"What about Devin? Is he still important to you?"

I sighed. "Of course he is, Carol. Devin's been the love of my life for twelve years. It doesn't suddenly stop. I'm at a crossroads that will decide if we have a future or not."

Jacinta set her glass on the table and stared me in the eye. "You mean if he's willing to let you take center stage."

I didn't respond. It was more than about career.

"Samina, if Devin wasn't committed, my boy would never have gone up against his father. Don't close off the possibilities. He loves you more than you could ever know."

"I love him too."

Dev was never one to stand up to his father, but today he defended me and supported me in a way he'd never done before.

"God," I said, releasing a sigh. "We are each other's escape from controlling fathers."

Carol smiled at me and patted my arm. "Then don't give up on him."

"I hope you're talking about me," Tyler said as he walked up and slid into the chair beside Carol.

Devin approached a few seconds later, staring at me with a look that told me he'd heard the tail end of the discussion.

He extended his hand, not taking his gaze from me or acknowledging anyone around him.

My heartbeat accelerated and a slow pulse began to throb in my core.

Licking my now-parched lips, I slid my palm over his and rose. His thumb grazed my skin, sending a shot of desire into every cell of my body.

"Where are you two off to?" Jacinta said from behind me.

Tyler answered, "To bump uglies, from the way he's eating her up."

The distinct sound of a smack echoed.

"Ow, Mom. That hurt."

"Tyler David Camden, leave them alone."

"Just you wait," Jacinta voiced. "One day we're going to have a field day at your expense."

"You're one to talk," Tyler said. "Besides, I would need a woman in my life for any of your evil plans to come to fruition."

Devin tucked a stray hair behind my ear and then said, "Let's go for a walk."

"Is that code for sex? Ow, Mom. Stop hitting me."

"Tyler, this is your last warning."

I couldn't help but laugh, which made a smile appear on Devin's face.

"It's a wonder you didn't drown him when you were younger." I gazed up at Devin.

He ran his thumb over my bottom lip. "I tried, but Mom wouldn't let me."

"I heard that," Tyler grumbled. "I swear. I get no respect in this family."

"Come on, let Mom deal with the Wonder Twins." Devin pulled me toward the river and then along a path leading away from the mansion.

So he wasn't using the long looks and notion of a walk as a guise to make our way back to our room.

I sighed and tried to mask my disappointment by focusing on the river.

God, I was pathetic. In less than forty-eight hours, he had me turned into a nymphomaniac who constantly craved his cock.

Who was I kidding? There wasn't a time I didn't want him to fuck me.

Devin smirked and shook his head.

"What?"

"You."

I jumped over a set of fallen branches, and then growled as my pumps dug into the ground.

"For someone who loves the outdoors and hiking, you don't seem to be enjoying it."

"I'm wearing three-inch heels, not sneakers. You should be happy I can walk in them at all over this uneven path."

"I have a solution."

I paused midstep. "I'm all ears."

He stepped toward me, and before I realized it, he'd thrown me over his shoulder. He took each of my shoes and tossed them to the side.

"Hey. Those were expensive."

"Baby, you have twenty other pairs. We'll pick them up on our way back."

"Bad Devin." I laughed. "Never touch a woman's Pradas."

I pinched his butt and then lingered to enjoy the feel of the firm muscles under my fingers.

He responded with a smack and squeeze to my bottom. "Behave."

"Are you planning on carrying me like this the rest of the way to wherever we are going?"

"Yes."

"Thanks, Mr. Vociferous."

"You're welcome, Mrs. Camden." His hand crept up the back of my dress, cupping my ass and then playing with the string of my thong, sliding it up and down his fingers.

Goosebumps prickled my skin.

"Stop it. We're out in the open." I lifted up and pulled at his hand, which only made him tug on my underwear harder.

"Devin," I said in a breathless whisper, and then a moan escaped my lips.

"We're here."

He set me on the steps of a cabin hidden among the trees. It was older, made of aged brick and wood. The landscaping was impeccably manicured and well established, telling me it was probably as old as the cabin.

"This is where you came when you studied for the bar," I said, glancing at him.

He remained quiet and watched me take in the house.

It was beautiful and had a charm only simple vintage homes had. The scent of pine blew through the trees, making me lift my face to the breeze.

"I love it," I said. "I take it this place was the original home before the mansion was built."

"It belonged to my mother's family. She inherited it but rarely came here with Dad's political career taking off in Louisiana. I'm happy Jacinta is putting the estate to use. Jacinta, Tyler, and I loved coming here to escape the political social scene back in New Orleans."

"I'm glad you showed me this place. I've always wanted to see the cabin you'd disappear to whenever you had to study."

He cupped my face and kissed my forehead. "I'm sorry I never brought you here before." There was a tinge of regret in his voice.

"I'm here now. Let's go inside."

We climbed the stairs and Dev unlocked the door. I was shocked to see how simple everything was inside. A small living room led to a tiny, almost minuscule kitchen, and a door in the back led to what I could only assume was the bedroom. There were knickknacks everywhere. I walked to the mantel lined with pictures. There were images of Carol and her sisters as teenagers, as well as Devin, Jacinta, and Tyler in various stages of growing up.

I traced the one of Dev standing on the dock, ready to jump into the Colorado River. He was so handsome, even then.

A throat cleared, snapping me from my perusal of the house.

My breath hitched as I turned to find Devin sitting on the couch with the same look he'd had in his eyes when he pulled me from my tea with Carol. His erection pushed against the seam of his pants, making my mouth water.

He crooked his finger at me and then pointed to the pillow on the floor between his legs.

Without thought, I moved toward him.

"Stop."

I paused midstep.

"Take off all your clothes first."

Slowly and meticulously, I slid the straps of my dress down my shoulders, letting the dress glide down the length of my body and pool at my feet.

"Keep going."

I unhooked my bra, revealing puckered nipples, and shimmied out of my sopping thong.

"Come here."

His raspy voice sent goosebumps over my skin.

I strolled toward him naked and barefoot. He offered me a hand and helped me lower myself onto the pillow.

We watched each other, our breaths a little shallow, and lust filled the air between us.

Sliding my palms up his fabric-covered thighs, I squeezed and molded the hard contours of his legs until I reached his belt. I pulled the leather from the loop and then unbuttoned and unzipped his pants, caressing his hard cock underneath.

"Take him out."

I followed his order, slowly freeing his cock from the confines of his pants.

The tip dripped with pre-cum, tempting me to have a taste. I licked the angry flared head, savoring his musky essence.

He fisted my hair. "Did I say to do that?"

I gave him a wicked grin and licked my lips. "No."

"Stroke me the way I like. Then I'll decide if you can suck my cock."

"Like this?" I smirked and cupped his balls with one hand as I gripped the base of his erection using the other. I glided slowly and firmly upward and downward a few times, using the cum dripping down the side as lube.

"Yes," he moaned, and his hold on me loosened.

"Or like this?"

I engulfed the head of his cock in my mouth and followed my fingers on their path downward.

"Oh, fuck. Sami," Devin cried out, giving me a sense of satisfaction at taking him by surprise.

As I traced the thick vein on the underside of his hard cock, I peeked up and saw his head thrown back and eyes closed tight.

I let him hit the back of my throat and then swallowed in the way that drove him crazy.

A deep, guttural rumble erupted from his mouth. The sound of his pleasure made the slickness from my pussy drip on the insides of my thighs, and I rocked back and forth, squeezing my legs tight to relieve some of my need.

I bobbed up and down in the rhythm that I knew he enjoyed.

"You're in so much trouble."

Pulling off for a second, I asked, "Doesn't that mean you want me to stop?"

He responded by cupping my face and bringing me back to his pulsing cock.

He took control, pumping in and out of my mouth. The feel of him using me for his desires pushed my body to scream for its own release.

I slid my fingers between my folds and strummed my aching clit.

Oh, yes.

My hip ground against my hand, trying to emulate the pace of Dev's thrusts. His fingers dug into my scalp, causing my eyes to water and sending me over. My knees buckled and I grabbed hold of Dev's legs. After a few more thrusts, his orgasm consumed him and he poured jets of hot cum down my throat.

I swallowed to match his release, taking in every drop until he finished. I licked him clean and Devin loosened his hold on my hair, and then I dropped my face onto his thigh.

I panted, trying to calm my breath, and a slow rumble came from him, reminding me of a cat who'd eaten a lot of cream.

Strike that. I was the one who had the cream.

I closed my eyes as Dev petted the side of my face.

"You've become feistier."

I lifted my head and questioned, "Is that a good thing or bad?"

"Sheathe your claws. I meant it as a compliment. Don't get me wrong, I love when you do everything I say, but this brat side is a turn-on."

"I'm a brat?" I crawled up his body, straddling him and making his softening cock twitch as I poised it between my folds.

He grabbed my hips and pulled me against his chest. "You proved my point."

He flipped me onto my back, caging me with his arms. He ran his tongue over my lips and then kissed me.

"You taste like me."

"I did have your monster cock in my mouth."

"I have other places it wants to go. Are you up for it?" His now-revived cock bobbed between us.

My man definitely had some master recovery. It's a wonder I could walk after one of our nonstop sex sessions.

"Don't we have to get back?"

"No. We're staying here."

I tried to push him up so I could sit, but he had me flat on my back again with my wrists pinned above my head in a matter of seconds.

I blew at a hair that had fallen over my face. "I'm sure your mom is expecting us for dinner. It's going to be embarrassing enough walking into the house with sex-tousled hair."

"I'm serious. We don't have to go back. Dinner is in the refrigerator and I moved our stuff here earlier."

I gazed up into his beautiful sculpted face. "Why?"

"Because this is my cabin and we aren't needed back until the morning." His voice grew serious. "Sami, I have so much to make up for and I wanted to start by spending time with you here, in one of my favorite places. A place I should have brought you to years ago."

Pulling my hands free of his hold, I cupped his cheeks. "As I said before, I'm here now."

The strain eased from his brow.

"Then I propose a game." He gave me a mischievous grin.

"What is it?"

He jumped off the couch and pulled me up, throwing me over his shoulder. "I call it hide and seek with the monster cock."

I smacked his butt. "Game on."

CHAPTER THIRTEEN

I woke to the sound of my phone buzzing.

Who could be calling me today? It was the Fourth, for crying out loud. A national holiday.

"Sami, answer the damn phone." Dev rolled over and covered his head with a pillow. "It's probably Jaci trying to fuck with us for leaving her with the family last night."

I picked up my phone. Shit, it was Tracy. That meant we had a situation. The Joneses threw one of the best Independence Day parties in Seattle. Unless it was a crisis, nothing would pull Tracy away from her family.

I slid out of bed, glanced at Dev, who was fast asleep again and looking sexy as hell, and then answered as I walked out of the room.

"What's wrong?"

"Good morning to you too. How do you know I'm calling because of a problem?"

"Tracy, it's—" I peeked at the clock on the wall, "—five thirty in the morning in Seattle. You'd only call this early if we were about to face a major problem."

"You're right. I found out Senators Sanders and Decker were spotted together in Key West this morning."

"That can't be a coincidence. Fuck. How the hell do they know I'm running? Who leaked this?"

"Your guess is as good as mine. You have never hidden your hatred for Decker Senior, but him helping a liberal incumbent makes no sense when his party is teetering to maintain control of the Senate."

"For the record, I don't hate him. I just want him to fall off a cliff or something."

"Same difference. The man you are about to challenge was seen with the man you consider your enemy and who happens to be your best friend's opponent. It only means they have something on you."

Dread crept in.

I sat on the couch and rested my elbows on my knees.

"This is bad."

"It's safe to say your secret is out. Sanders is an ass on a good day, but you're a viable threat. He's going to go for the jugular. Is there anything he can use against you? We have to prepare for damage control before anything is made public."

I had to get it out in one go, and I could handle Tracy's reaction.

"Decker hired a reporter, Spencer Miller, to break into my house and take nude pictures of me. He ended up taking the pictures but also tried to corner me. I kicked him in the balls and broke his nose, giving me enough time to press the panic button in the bathroom and get away. The police arrested him, but I realized a little too late that he'd uploaded the images to a cloud server, giving Decker direct access to them."

"Hold on. When did this happen and why didn't you tell me?"

I pressed my fingers to my forehead. "It was something I wanted to keep quiet. I felt ashamed."

"Why? You did nothing wrong."

I blew out a deep breath. "Tracy, I'm the image of a ball-busting attorney. I've represented a shock jock, celebrities, and politicians. If word got out, Sanders would twist the facts so I ended up looking like a whore who asked for it. This could have ramifications for my family and Dev's family, including their careers."

"What you're saying is that you care less about how it affected you as a woman violated than other people. Isn't your platform one of fighting against the establishment and accepted practices in politics? You went toe to toe with those who tried to shred my reputation. Don't you deserve the same kind of defense? Fight for yourself."

I waited a moment before I responded.

Oh God, I was doing that exact thing I'd tried to keep Jacinta from doing. It was so much easier when I viewed it from the outside and pretended what happened to me wasn't as bad.

It didn't matter what industry, there were countless

victims of those who used their power and status to ruin others as a way to get what they wanted.

A chill shook my body as did a new sense of determination and worry.

I couldn't let Miller's actions victimize me anymore, and without a doubt, I wasn't going to let someone else fight my battles for me, especially not Richard. He would spin it to his benefit, not mine.

"I'm going to fight him, Tracy. I'm going to make Sanders wish he never joined forces with Decker."

"Good, now we need to pinpoint how Decker got the information about you running for Senate."

All of the sudden it hit me. "My God, I think Miller took pictures of the candidacy paperwork that night. The incident happened the day after you stopped by with the forms. And..." I scraped a hand down my face.

"...And that's the only way anyone outside of our circle would know your plans," she said, finishing my sentence. "That piece of shit bastard. That's the reason he uploaded the pictures. He found a political gold mine when he broke into your house."

"When do you think Sanders will release the pictures to the media?"

"I expect it within the next twenty-four hours. The moment Sanders learned you were considering a run against him, he'd view you as a credible threat, especially with your popularity at an all-time high and his at the lowest it has been in twenty years. He's going to look for any way possible to discredit you."

"That bastard would use my violation as a way to defame my character."

"I told you from the beginning, politics is ruthless, but for a woman, it is twice as brutal. For political capital, my challenger accused me of sleeping my way to the top of my law firm. Those allegations not only hurt my reputation, but my family. I fought back with your help. Now it's your turn."

"I guess it has to happen."

She knew what I meant without me saying it. "Yes."

"When?"

"Tomorrow morning at the latest. I'll file the paperwork you left with Tara and by eight a.m. it will be official."

A lump formed in my stomach. The ball was rolling.

I wanted to take back control of my life, and now I was getting what I wished. Only it was happening leaps and bounds faster than I expected. I had hoped for a few more weeks to work on my marriage and figure out the next steps before making the announcement.

Oh God. How was Devin going to react?

"I'm scared, Tracy. What if..."

She cut me off. "Stop worrying. He'll stand with you. He loves you. Why do you think my niece is such a bitch to you?"

"Who's that?" I asked, and then it hit me. "Are you talking about Judge McGregor?"

"How did you not know this? She looks like a younger version of me."

"I don't keep up with your family tree."

"Are you telling me you didn't investigate the woman who your husband took to a charity gala?"

I felt a growl form in the back of my throat, and it required all my willpower to keep it in. "No. I was more concerned about the demise of my marriage and the fact I lived in our brand-new house alone."

"You should be happy to know that Karen said she had an absolutely miserable time."

"Why is that?" My mood lightened a little, and I moved to the kitchen, started the water kettle, and pulled out the French press, adding in a few scoops of coffee.

"Karen reported that the moment he saw you walk in with Veer George, he about lost it. He wanted to leave before the announcer introduced the first auction item."

I remembered that night vividly. After Devin told me he couldn't go with me to the gala since it could hurt his career, I'd called Veer. He never failed me and flew up for the event. I couldn't deny that I had a great time with him, but it wasn't the same as going with Devin.

When Veer dropped me at home later that evening, I encountered a very agitated Devin, who threw me over his shoulder and fucked me until I barely could speak my name.

"Dev has no right to be jealous." The kettle beeped, and I poured the water over the coffee grounds. "For crying out loud, Veer's like a brother to me."

"Well, your husband thought otherwise. And that was the day Karen discovered you two had a thing going."

Now I understood her disdain for me. She had to have felt used.

I shot a look toward the bedroom door. *Oh Devin, you break hearts without knowing it.*

He was so easy to love. He had a way about him that drew people in. I'd fallen for him the very day we'd met, twelve years earlier when I'd roomed with Jacinta at Stanford.

I'd come home to change before I went to a yoga class and to my surprise, the sexiest man I'd ever seen was sitting on my couch, wearing a Harvard Law T-shirt and watching TV. He didn't notice me until I'd made some sarcastic comment about an enemy in Stanford territory. The moment our eyes locked, I was a goner.

"Damn. I just thought of something funny," Tracy said with a laugh, snapping me from my thoughts.

"What's that?"

"Jacinta Camden is about to get another notch in her candidate collecting belt. First, she enters the race for Senate, then she convinces Veer George to run for governor, and now you're going to make an official announcement. I wish I were in her shoes. She's going to get all the credit for influencing you to run."

"I'm glad my personal and political angst is a competition between you and Jaci," I muttered as I filled my cup to the brim and took a sip of the piping-hot brew. "Everyone is going to lose their minds when I break the news tonight and tell them why I'm making it official. Shit.

It will have to wait until all the guests leave, and that will be close to midnight."

"It's the way it works, Samina. Your family's approval isn't going to change the course you're taking. All I can say is enjoy today, and get ready for a roller-coaster ride."

"Not helping, whatsoever."

Tracy chuckled. "I'll call you in the morning. Stop worrying about Devin."

"That's easy for you to say. I'm the one who has to inform my husband what we're planning."

"That's marriage," she said and hung up.

I placed my phone on the counter and took a deep breath.

Oh God. What was I going to do? I had to tell him.

Last night, we'd agreed to talk each step of our lives out. This was our chance to get it right, to fix the mess we'd created of our relationship. Now I'd made the official decision to run without consulting him.

Would he still support me when I was about to do to him the exact thing I was so angry with him for doing to me?

I released a deep breath and rested my face against the hard surface of the kitchen counter.

This was my life now. A game of strategy, a chess match where I had to outmaneuver the sitting king. The second the papers were filed, Senator Anthony Sanders would declare war on me, and he would use nude pictures of me to shame me. Everyone I knew would see them. My family would see them. What was Mummy going to think?

Would she blame me as I expected Papa would? I could almost hear Richard telling me to get over it. But Carol didn't deserve the media spectacle thrown on her.

Oh God, Jacinta. She'd blame herself. I'd have to make sure she understood this time I was going to fight for her and me.

I lifted my head to rest my face in my hands.

I'd better wake Dev and give him the not-so-good news.

"That view of your naked, round ass is priceless. A man always wants to see his sexy wife in her birthday suit first thing in the morning."

I stood, turning to face a nude Devin, and quickly wiped the tear running down my face.

"Baby, what's wrong?" The playfulness of his mood disappeared as he approached me.

"Dev, I have something to tell you."

He stared at me and then ran a thumb along my damp cheek.

"Does it have to do with the pictures or the election?"

"Both," I answered. "It's going to make you into a public figure as much as I am."

He continued to gaze into my eyes before he spoke. "I don't care. Not right now."

"This is important. I have to prepare you."

"I said, I don't care." He cupped my face. "You can tell me later. Right now, I have to take care of you. Tell me what you need."

My lips trembled as I gripped his forearms. In all our

years together, he'd never put a critical discussion on the back burner.

He was giving me an out from talking about it. At least for the moment. I wanted to lose myself in him. To go back to last night, when it was just the two of us in a cabin in the woods by the river.

"Make love to me. Don't let me think."

"With pleasure." He lips sealed over mine.

His kiss intoxicated me, taking my worry and replacing it with a desire only he could satisfy.

Soon our world would turn upside down and put our marriage to the test.

He fisted my hair, jerking my head back. "Focus on this. On me. Not on what's inside your head."

He slammed his mouth against mine again, sandwiching me between him and the counter. His erection was a firm rod between us.

The crisp hair on his chest rubbed against my nipples, causing them to pebble. The exquisite sensation made me cry out and made my arousal drip onto my thighs.

He used the opportunity to trail his tongue along the curve of my throat, down the valley between my breasts, and then to one tight, straining bud, which grew even harder with contact. He circled, teased, and laved until my legs couldn't hold me up anymore.

I gripped the edge of the counter before I lost balance. Devin smirked and transferred his attention to my other aching nipple. His teeth bit into the sensitive flesh.

"Dev," I cried out, and my pussy clenched from the pleasure-pain.

His mouth was magic. He made my flesh scream for attention and my pussy cream for anything and everything he had in store for me.

He lifted me against his body, carrying me to the breakfast table and then setting me on the edge. I tried to wrap my legs around him, but he pushed me onto my back. He journeyed lower, licking, kissing, and nibbling. Once he reached my quivering pussy, he spread my knees, settling my feet on each of his shoulders.

He tongued my sopping slit, back and forth, not going any deeper. My fingers clenched the beveled edge of the wood, and my legs shook.

I looked down to catch his gaze. He lifted a brow, telling me he knew what I desired but wasn't going to give it to me until he was ready.

I released a low growl as he continued his teasing torture and blew on my pulsing clit. I moved my hands to my swollen breasts, cupping them and pinching the tips.

A rumble of satisfaction vibrated against my pussy lips, and I opened my eyes to find him watching me.

At that moment, he pushed between my pussy lips and straight into my core. His hands gripped my ass, bringing me closer to his exploring mouth. He circled my clit with his thumb and thrust it deep inside my clenching walls. My pussy quivered with each flick and stroke.

I soaked his face with my desire, wanting nothing more than to go over the edge.

I had to wait.

God. Why was he making me wait?

"Please, Dev. Please," I begged. "Let me come."

"Come for me, baby," he murmured against my aching core.

My body responded on command. I screamed his name, clenching my pussy and my eyes tight. My body spasmed to his evil, delicious mouth.

I rode out my release, delirious with nothing but the need for pleasure.

Before I could come down, he had me rising again. I thrashed my head side to side and gripped his hair in a tight hold.

My second orgasm rose almost immediately, making my mind cloud once again.

"Oh, I don't think so. You didn't ask permission." He pulled back, wiping his wet mouth against my inner thigh.

Protesting, I tried to hold him to me. "No, don't leave me hanging."

He slipped from my fingers and stood, ignoring my words.

His hard, angry cock dripped like a faucet and gave me a bit of satisfaction to see his tortured state. He pulled me toward him, brought my legs around his waist, and then lifted me into his arms.

Devin strode to the bedroom and laid me on the bed. He crawled over me, caging my body under his and holding my legs together with his thighs.

He gripped my jaw and peered down at me with eyes filled with lust and domination. "Who gives the commands, baby? Who holds the reins?"

"Me." I jerked my face, but he held it firm.

"Wrong answer." He lowered his body, grazing his beautiful, hard cock along the valley of my aching pussy and making me arch toward him. "If you want this, you have to answer truthfully."

"Dammit, Devin. Fuck me, please."

I gripped his shoulder and dug my nails in. He released my face and captured my wrists, pinning them above my head.

"That wasn't very nice, brat." He chuckled into my ear and then bit the lobe as the flared, angry head of his erection pressed and dripped on my clit. "I can keep this up as long as you want. Now tell me, who's in charge?"

I panted, trying to focus on his face and not the rod teasing my pussy.

This was a game we'd played over and over throughout the years. We both knew Devin had a hold on me no one else ever would. No matter how it was in public, he'd always taken the reins in private. And I'd never had a problem with it.

My desires were a walking contradiction. I wanted control of my life but needed Dev to be in charge in the bedroom.

"Come on, baby. Give me the answer, and I'll give you what you want."

His cock rimmed the entrance of my pussy, pushing in and out in shallow thrusts and teasing my screaming clit.

I tried my best to pull my legs apart and angle him into my body, but Dev only squeezed his thighs tighter around me and prevented me from moving my lower body.

He pushed in farther and then pulled out to the tip, rubbing his flared head back and forth along the apex of my lower lips and making my clit throb to a point where I thought I'd lose my mind.

"You don't seem to want it very badly."

He lifted up, releasing his hold on me. I grabbed him before he could move too far.

He wouldn't leave me like this. He couldn't. Maybe I should have given him what he wanted, and then he'd fuck me the way I liked.

"Dev, please," I pleaded.

He held my gaze, smiled, and pulled me onto his lap, positioning me against his erect cock but not where I wanted it. My pussy quivered as my arousal dripped onto his legs.

"All you have to do is answer a simple question." He fisted my hair, angling my face toward his, and kissed me, but pulled back as I deepened it, and peered into my eyes. "Who's in charge, baby?"

His voice softened, and the game was over as fast as it started. I cupped his face, running my thumb over his cheek.

"Who has memorized every gorgeous dip and curve of

this body?" He ran a hand up my naked back. "Who's the one who doesn't deserve you but will love you until his dying breath?"

"Oh, Dev."

"Answer me."

I wrapped my arms around his neck. "You. It will always be you."

He sealed our mouths in response. This time the kiss was filled with need on both our parts. He lowered me back onto the bed, one hand kneading my hip as the other cupped a breast. I spread my thighs to accommodate him, and in one swift move, he was deep inside me. Everything in me rippled to life. My pussy clenched and my nipples pebbled into harder peaks.

He stared into my eyes as he moved in and out, rubbing the sensitive spot deep inside my sopping core. My pussy quickened, and my back bowed against him.

"We're going to make it." Thrust. "We're going to fix the mess we made." Thrust. "And no matter what is thrown our way." Thrust. "We will stand together. I love you, Sami. I'm not going to let you down ever again."

His words released the lump I felt in the pit of my stomach. He would be my rock as we moved into the uncertain future. I loved him so much.

At that moment he changed his rhythm from soft to hard, pushing me to the place I'd begged him to take me.

This man unhinged me, consuming every part of my mind and body.

My core quivered one last time as an avalanche of emotion and release beat down on me. I squeezed and pulsed around Devin's cock, saying words that made no sense. I continued to contract around him until he called my name and collapsed, filling me with his release and his love.

CHAPTER FOURTEEN

A few hours later, after a long, hot shower, where Devin and I enjoyed his phenomenal abilities of recovery, I stood along the banks of the Colorado River, where Jacinta's party was in full swing. Every politician, socialite, and celebrity who wanted to be in the society magazines was in attendance.

The moment we'd arrived at the house, Devin and I had separated. Richard had taken Tyler and Devin to meet prominent members of his party and Carol had done her best to introduce me to everyone and anyone she believed had any useful political pull.

I appreciated her support, but the majority of people wanted to discuss my clients, my new celebrity status, and the fact that I was now on the cover of five popular magazines, including one that named me one of the top single professionals in Washington and the United States. A topic I was positive had reached Devin's ears.

For the past thirty minutes, every time I glanced toward the balcony of Jacinta's house, I'd caught him watching me.

The possessiveness of Dev's gaze made my pulse jump and would add to the rumors swirling around the party about us. Several people had alluded to my closeness to the Camden family but no one had directly asked me about it.

"Excuse me, Samina. You don't mind if I call you Samina, do you? Ms. Kumar sounds so formal."

I turned as Veronica Jane Cartwright approached me with her sister, Jill. Just the sight of Veronica made my green-eyed monster want to rear its ugly head. She was a leggy Amazon who loved to parade around all the elite circles acting like an intellectual. She also thought my husband was her living boy toy.

She gave me one of the fake smiles she was known for and took a sip of her cocktail.

"No, of course not. That is my name."

She was all bottled blond and teased hair. The quintessential Louisiana debutante, who came from the right family and pedigree. She was everything I wasn't. The kind of woman Devin was expected to marry.

I was sure the only reason she'd sought me out was that she'd heard the rumors about my marriage. We'd encountered each other before, and she hadn't given me a second glance.

Now I had to smile and act like the well-bred daughter of a billionaire I was and not punch her in the face the moment she said something snide as she was reputed to do.

"What's it like to represent celebrities? I'm sure you have all kinds of gossip."

I looked to her side and caught Jacinta watching me. She cringed and mouthed, "Sorry."

Girl owed me big time for dealing with Veronica.

Samina, this is only the beginning. You're about to jump into politics. Kissing babies and pretending to like people will become part of the job.

"It isn't all the tabloids make it out to be. They are normal people, for the most part."

"Oh, come on. I'm sure you have some great stories to share." Jill was the polar opposite of her sister. Beautiful in a more natural way, and her smile was genuine. The kind that could draw anyone in and make them feel important.

"Attorney-client privilege. I don't disclose anything private about the people I represent."

"What about Clint Bassett's push to have you run for office?"

I laughed. "That is something my former client is using to get ratings. Don't take any of it as truth."

Shit. I had just given a politician's answer, a lie and the truth at the same time. I guessed being a litigator gave me practice.

I lifted my wrist to glance at my watch. Fifteen minutes and Dev was supposed to get me.

"Oh my God. Look at those rings," Jill exclaimed as she snatched my hand into hers. "I've never seen a pink diamond wedding band before. And look at that solitaire. It has to be at least five carats. Veronica, do you see this? You have a man with exquisite taste."

I cringed. I loved my rings but drawing attention to them when Devin and I hadn't appeared in public as a couple outside of Devin's statement to the reporter was uncomfortable.

From a distance, I saw Dev smirk in my direction. I narrowed my eyes at him and he lifted his cocktail as if saying, "Glad it's you and not me."

"I guess the rumors are true." Veronica inspected my ring with a frown. "Who's the lucky man?"

Like she had no clue. I'd heard enough people making whispered comments to tell me they'd listened to the tabloid reports about Devin and me.

"He's here somewhere. I'm sure you'll meet him later tonight." I kept my answer vague. "I heard you've been dating one of the Texans players."

Her face lit up as I moved the conversation to her. "Oh, you know how it is. Athletes are perfect to practice on, but I'm holding out for someone else."

I could guess the man she was waiting on.

"Do I know this gentleman?"

"Devin Camden, of course," she said as if that had been a stupid question, and her glare could have killed me. "We've been seeing each other on and off for years. Our families are very close."

Veronica grabbed a drink off a passing tray and chugged the contents of the glass. Hope she realized the cocktails Jacinta served at her parties could lay a three-hundred-pound man on his ass.

"Veronica, I think that ship has sailed." Jill lifted a brow. "Rumor has it that he's been in a secret marriage for years. You're close to the family. Do you know who she is?"

I kept my face composed, not giving away anything. "Everyone will meet his wife sometime during the evening."

"I'm sure I'll like her very much. Devin has great taste." Jill smiled up at me, reiterating to me how different she was compared to her fake sister. "Is she from down south or a Seattle girl? I bet she's gorgeous, like you."

"I wouldn't say she's a Southern girl, but she isn't from Seattle either."

Veronica handed her glass to a passing waiter and then asked, "Is she foreign? Is that why he kept her hidden?"

Jill nearly spit out her drink and not-so-subtly elbowed Veronica in the side.

"I'm sure they have their reasons for wanting their privacy. I can respect that," Jill assured her sister, who was frowning. "Wouldn't you agree, Veronica?"

I could see myself being friends with Jill. She played the social game but never crossed the line. She reminded me of Jacinta. Too bad her sister was sour-faced next to us.

"I suppose. What I want to know is, how does she compare to me? What about her made Devin marry her?"

The woman's underhanded digs were getting me to the point of retaliating. Veronica knew I was Devin's wife, and no matter what she hoped, it wasn't going to change anytime soon.

Jill set a gentle hand on my arm as if to keep me calm. "He's obviously in love with her."

Veronica snorted, making me see red. She had to be drunk, that could be the only answer.

I'd thought Southern belles were poised to perfection and held in their insults until they were in private circles.

I'd better leave before I said something I shouldn't and possibly deck her hard enough to knock her into the water.

"If you'll excuse me, I need to check when my brother will arrive."

"One second." Veronica grasped my arm, stopping me from leaving her. "I have a message you can relay to Devin's wife."

Jill pried Veronica's fingers from me. "Veronica. Let Samina see to her family. We can talk later. Maybe on the riverboat."

She ignored her sister. "Hold on with both hands. Secret wives can be easily replaced."

Jill gasped and pulled on her sister, giving me an apologetic look. "Ver, I think it's time we had some water. I don't want you to get seasick on the boat. Samina, please excuse us."

"I know what I'm saying."

"Veronica, I agree with Jill. It's time to switch to something that will clear your mind. I would hate for you to have to explain to your father why you were raising your voice to the daughter of one of his biggest donors."

"Is that a threat, Samina Kumar? Fine." She huffed. "Just make sure you...Devin's tramp...knows I plan to make it very difficult for Devin to forget me. I wouldn't be surprised if I was his date to the Governor's Ball again and to every other event in the future."

A throbbing started in my head, and I clenched my fists.

Oh, this bitch was about to get me arrested.

Before I could respond, Veer slipped an arm around my waist. "Hello, ladies."

He inclined his head at Jill and Veronica.

"I hope you don't mind me taking Sam away. Jacinta wanted to introduce her colleagues to her best friend and sister-in-law."

I barely had any time to notice the ladies' reactions before Veer tugged me forward.

"You did that on purpose. You used Jacinta's name as a way to rescue me from Her Royal Bitchiness."

"Guilty." He smirked.

"Thank you. I was about to commit a homicide."

"Anyone with eyes could see Veronica was five seconds from floating in the river. The whole family has issues."

"Jill isn't so bad."

"She's the exception. Probably has to do with the fact she's only Veronica's stepsister and has lived overseas for the last ten years."

"Why do you know so much about her?"

"I'm not a stalker, if that's what you're thinking."

"The thought never crossed my mind." I laughed up at

him and followed him down the path toward some of our friends from Houston.

"You're such a brat. The reason I know so much about Jill is that she manages my family's London offices and is married to one of my European partners."

"At least she only has to deal with Veronica in small doses. I'd hate to see what the witch was like as a child."

"Come on, shorty. Where's your husband? Shouldn't he be the one to keep you out of the clutches of the evil witch?"

"He's over there, staring daggers at me."

Dev glowered at me from his position in the middle of the crowd.

"No, the knives are pointed in my direction. I've got my arm around his woman."

"Whatever, he's been over there for the past hour instead of with me. I'm going to enjoy the company of my almost-brother."

"Give him a break, Sam. This is his sister's party and she going to run for Senate this year. He has to help her make connections."

I scanned the area around Devin again. People surrounded him and Jacinta on all sides. I could tell both of them wanted an escape, but with so many people talking, they weren't getting away anytime soon.

"You're right. I'm an ass."

"You said it. Not me."

I shoved him on the shoulder as we laughed.

"Let's go mingle and make fun of everyone in a

language no one else understands."

"Samina, you are wrong on so many levels."

An hour later, I left Veer to his parents, who'd just arrived, and sneaked into the kitchen for a quick break from the crowd outside.

Caterers and servers shuffled around the large room, preparing dish after dish. Jacinta had something for everyone, including Indian dishes for Veer's parents, who were vegetarian.

I loved that girl. She was not only a brilliant litigator but a top-of-the-line hostess.

I walked around the large island, enjoying all the delicious smells. Well, except the meat. It smelled too pungent.

I moved to a tray of naan, grabbed a piece to nibble on, and then had the urge to use the bread to scoop up some paneer tikka masala, a dish I hadn't made in ages.

I used to make all kinds of Indian dishes, especially those from the region of Gujarat, where my family originated. Over the past year, I never seemed to have time and then when I did, I was too tired to cook and ordered takeout which left me disappointed and hungry. Restaurant food never tasted as good as the homemade dishes my mom taught me to make.

"Here you go, Ms. Kumar." The chef handed me a plate filled with samples of all the Indian dishes. "Ms.

Camden had a feeling you'd sneak in here. She said you've barely eaten today."

"Thank you." I took my plate to the breakfast nook in the back of the room.

I dug in, and before I realized it, I'd all but licked the plate clean.

Whoever Jacinta hired to make the food was a rock star. It was almost to Anya Kumar standards, and comparing anyone to my mom's level of cooking was a compliment.

I missed her so much.

Ashur had said he was going to do his best to get Mummy to come, but I doubted it would happen. Papa had a tight hold on her, and she never did anything without his permission.

At least I'd get to see my big brother.

I got up to set my plate in the sink and then ran upstairs to make a quick pit stop in my old room to brush my teeth. Jacinta always kept extra hygiene supplies in the medicine cabinets. Indian food had a very aromatic scent that I loved. However, not everyone shared my opinion.

After freshening up, I made my way down the hall leading to the front of the house. Ashur was due to arrive within the next half hour, and I wanted to be outside when his car approached.

Just as I passed the library, someone pulled me into a nearby room and covered my mouth with their hand.

"Don't make a sound. I have something to discuss with you."

CHAPTER FIFTEEN

I gasped as Dev's hand slid from over my mouth.

"Devin, have you lost your mind?" I admonished, but the look in his eyes had my heartbeat accelerating. "No. Don't even think about it. Haven't you gotten enough? You fucked me three times this morning."

He took a deep breath, his chest expanding as he scanned me from head to toe. He lingered on my breasts in a way that made my nipples pebble and my pussy flood with need.

"You are mine." He pushed me hard against the wall and cupped my crotch.

His touch shot through me like a fire igniting. I held my breath in hopes of pushing back the desire pulsing to life inside my body.

"This is mine. Don't ever let Veer or any man think they have a chance with you."

How could he be jealous of Veer? How could Devin not understand that the only man I'd ever want was him?

"Veer is my friend. I think of him as a brother. How many times do I need to tell you this? Nothing has ever happened between us and it never will."

He gripped the bottom of my dress, jerking it up, and then ripped my underwear, making me gasp.

"You can't fuck me here. We're in a housekeeper's closet. Anyone could come by or hear us."

Dev ignored me and flipped me around until my front pressed against the wall.

The telltale sound of his belt and zipper echoed in the small space.

My heart thundered in my ears as my pussy swelled and creamed, wanting Dev's cock to fill me to the brim.

"I will fuck you anywhere I damn please. This pussy curves to the shape of my dick. I think you need a reminder." His fingers slid between my folds, teased my now aching clit while spreading my desire up and down my slit. "From the way you're dripping, I'd say you want it as bad as I do."

Before I could respond, he impaled me with one hard shove, making my body arch against the wall.

"Oh God, Dev," I cried out.

"Does it feel good, baby?" He rolled his hips, pressing against the sensitive spot deep inside.

I panted, "Yes."

"Then don't ever forget that I am the only man in your

life." He pulled out to the tip of his flared head and slammed back into me.

"You have no room to say anything. That bitch Veronica has her nasty sights set on you. She talked about you as if you belonged to her." I tried to push him off, but it only made him pound into me harder.

"Are you jealous, my love?"

I growled, hating how much I needed him. "Of course I'm jealous. I'm also hurt. How would you like it if I were photographed with another man and then the society magazines posted an article about him as my potential future spouse?"

"I'd hate it," he said against my ear and continued to pound me, pressing my sensitive nipples against the wall. "Just as I want to rip the throats out of the editors that put you on the covers of those magazines. You are not single. You are my fucking wife."

"I rest my case, Your Honor," I gritted out, hating that I couldn't get enough of him. "And for the record. I hate that social climber."

I should be so angry at him for manhandling me, but all my body wanted to do was scream for release.

"Sami, I don't want her. I want the woman who makes my dick hard by just breathing in my direction. The woman who loves me so much that she's put up with my bullshit for years. The very woman whose pussy I'm pummeling with my cock and plan to fill with my babies."

"Tell that to Veronica. She thinks she can make you

forget all about your wife. The wife you haven't introduced to anyone, by the way. She's already planning to be your date for next year's Governor's Ball. She thinks I'm insignificant."

Dev grasped my throat in a light hold and tilted my head back so our eyes could lock.

Lust and need filled his gaze.

"Nothing can make me forget my wife. Veronica is more plastic than a Barbie. I have a thing for an Indian brunette with natural features, a fiery temper, and a body I could get lost in for hours. You're the only woman I plan to be seen with for the rest of my life."

His words made my heart skip a beat, and the irritation I felt at the conversation I'd had with Veronica disappeared. But he had to know I'd never put up with his crap ever again.

"If you ever take another woman to any more events, I will never forgive you. I don't care if nothing ever happened with them. Don't ever think of coming back home again. We'll be divorced before you know what hit you."

"Are we really talking about you divorcing me while I'm fucking you? I must not be giving it to you good enough."

Dev's pace changed, and all I could do was focus on the sensations coursing through my body.

"More," I cried out. "Harder, please Dev. I'm almost there."

Dev released his hold on my neck, kissed my shoulder,

and then covered my hands, pressing against the wall with his.

"Fuck yourself against me, baby. Show me what only my cock can satisfy."

I pushed back, meeting each thrust for thrust.

My body heated and pussy quickened.

Right there, yes. Right there.

I threw my head back as my orgasm surged forward, coursing through every pore in my body like a bomb detonating.

My pussy contracted hard, clamping down on Dev's pulsing cock and trying to draw out the sensation longer.

"You're not done yet. I need to hear my name on your lips at least two more times," he whispered into my ear.

And I did, again and again.

I tried to say something but could only moan—verbalizing my feelings wasn't possible.

Dev was still thrusting inside me, and then a few seconds after my third orgasm, he came, calling out my name and shooting his cum deep inside my still-trembling pussy.

I rested my face on the wall, barely able to remember my name, while Dev leaned against my back, trying to catch his breath.

"Oh God. What have you done to me?"

"I've just shown you to whom you belong. And remember this, if you flirt with any more men, I'll do it again."

A giggle bubbled up and I shook my head. "You are

absolutely insane, Devin Camden. No wonder I love you so much."

"Say that again."

"What?" I asked over my shoulder, but Dev pulled out of my body and turned me to face him.

"Tell me again how you feel. Tell me again that you love me and I haven't killed what we shared by neglecting you. That I'm not pushing you toward the man who's perfect for you."

My face softened as I cupped his cheek. The uncertainty in his eyes made me realize how much he feared I'd leave him for Veer. Both Jacinta and V were right—Devin did view V as competition.

"Dev, I've told you over and over."

"No, you talked about loving me. You haven't said the words to me."

"I love you, Devin James Camden. You are the only man I have loved and will ever love."

He kissed first my forehead, followed by my nose, and last my lips, before he whispered, "You are my everything, Sami. Love doesn't describe what I feel for you."

"Oh Devin." I leaned my head against him, savoring the feel of this moment.

A knock sounded on the door, making me groan.

"I know you're in there," Jacinta shouted with a hint of annoyance in her voice.

"Jaci, go away," I said as I pulled back from Devin and tried to fix my dress.

"You have a cabin for the shit you're doing in there.

Dammit, there are at least five bedrooms upstairs you could have used. Now I'm going to have to sanitize the housekeeper's storage closet."

"Was there a purpose for seeking us out?" Dev tucked himself back into his pants. "Or are you just being an annoying little sister?"

"You need to get your asses out onto the patio. People are noticing your disappearances, especially Mom."

"We'll be there in a few." I scowled at Devin. "Dammit, Dev. I'm wrinkled. Why do you have this need to bunch up my clothes all the time? Ashur is about to arrive, and I look a hot mess."

"No, you look like you were thoroughly fucked by your husband."

"The last thing my brother wants to see is his sister sex-tousled and flushed."

He pushed my hands away from the hem of my dress, lifted it back up, and used my torn underwear to clean up the stickiness between my legs.

When he was satisfied, he pulled the flowery fabric down, straightened his clothes, and then tucked my wet thong into the pocket of his slacks.

"Now you are presentable."

"Thank you."

He looked up from buckling his belt and smiled. "It was my pleasure."

My heart skipped a beat. "You are too good looking for your own good."

"Are you complaining?" His cheeks reddened.

It always seemed to embarrass him when I mentioned his looks.

"No. What woman doesn't want a man who looks almost as good as her?" I joked and stood on tiptoes to kiss him.

At that moment the door slammed open, and an annoyed Jacinta walked in with her arms crossed and a scowl on her face.

"Seriously, you two have got to get down there. Ash's car is approaching the house." Jacinta grabbed my arm and yanked me from Dev. "Sam, you look like you've been freshly fucked."

"That's because she has." Dev wedged his way between Jacinta and me, sliding his hands around our waists. "And I'll do it again if you don't keep your gubernatorial candidate away from her."

"He's her family. Honestly, you need to get over this jealousy when it comes to Veer George."

"That's what I told him," I said. "Besides, I think Jacinta is the one he wants to do delicious, dirty things to."

Dev paused. "Someone kill me now."

"At least you're thinking about Veer and Jaci instead of me. Can you imagine it? An independent with liberal tendencies and a conservative, getting it on. They'd make politically hybrid babies."

"Sam, stop before you give him a coronary."

"Did you notice she didn't object to the image I painted about her and V?"

"Sami?"

"Yes, love?"

"Stop talking. You aren't helping."

"Sorry. I was only trying to make a point."

"On that note, I need to check on the caterers. Head out and tell Mom I'll be there in a minute." Jacinta slipped out of Dev's arm and went down the hallway to the kitchen.

The second Dev and I walked onto the patio leading down to the shore, multiple sets of eyes focused on us.

"You know all the single ladies and half the married ones are going to hate me and have visions of throwing me overboard the moment we leave the dock."

"The only woman whose happiness I give two shits about is yours." He cupped my face and kissed my forehead. "Come on. I see Ash's car."

We took the steps leading to the driveway and joined Carol and Tyler.

"Where'd you two disappear to, Mr. and Mrs. Camden?" Tyler said it loud enough to be in earshot of everyone around us.

"I had to show Sami some rooms she hadn't seen before."

Tyler snorted. "That's why your shirt and Samina's dress are wrinkled."

Carol popped Tyler on the back of the head. "Tyler David Camden. You know better than to comment on their clothes when we're surrounded by company. I have no idea where I went wrong with you boys."

"Hey, what did I do? I'm merely escorting my wife to

meet her brother." Dev pretended he was offended.

"You know what you did. Hello, Samina dear."

"Hello."

"Word of advice." She scanned my attire and shook her head while glaring at Dev. "Don't give in so easily. Make him work for it. How are you ever going to get your way if you don't leave him wanting on occasion? How do you think the senator and I made it through forty years?"

"Mom, people can hear you." Jacinta sounded scandalized as she approached.

"Seriously," Tyler added. "The last thing I want to think of is you and Dad having sex."

"You can't possibly think the tooth fairy brought you into existence?"

Tyler groaned. "Stork, Mom, not tooth fairy."

"Same difference, they're both made up. The point I was trying to make is, don't put out unless Devin makes it worth your while."

"I do, Mom. That's why she's standing here with a well-satisfied sex glow."

"Devin, honey."

"Yes, Mom."

"Shut up."

"Yes, ma'am."

I loved this woman. She could make any situation fun.

I grinned as the limo door opened, ready to hug my brother, but immediately my smile vanished and tears filled my eyes.

"Mummy."

CHAPTER SIXTEEN

I ran to the car, hugging the beautiful woman with long black hair and kind eyes who stepped out.

"*Mari Dikri*, I missed you so much." She hugged me so tight that I couldn't help but let the tears free. Five years without seeing her, without her hugs or her little quirks that made me feel loved.

She smelled of jasmine and lilies, the scent I associated with love and my childhood.

"Oh, Mummy. I'm so happy you're here." I held on to her and cried for the next few minutes, not caring if I was making a spectacle of myself in front of all the guests.

Finally, when we pulled apart, I glanced behind me and found both Carol and Jacinta dabbing at their eyes.

"Do I get any love or does Mummy get to hog you?"

I stepped out of Mummy's arms and turned toward my brother, but noticed my father standing behind Ashur.

I peeked at Dev, who gave me a nod of encouragement.

"Ash," I whispered and let him engulf me in his giant arms. "Thank you."

"It wasn't me. The man behind you is the reason she's here. The reason they're both here."

I looked into Dev's eyes. This was what he'd been doing in Houston. Not meeting with potential donors. He was trying to convince my parents to come see me. I couldn't imagine what it was like for Devin to stand in front of my father after all the hell Papa put us through.

I love you, I mouthed to him, making him smile at me.

I stepped out of Ashur's arms and approached my father.

"Papa."

He looked older, with more gray in his hair and lines on his face. He seemed a bit more fragile than the formidable man I knew growing up, who'd tried to control my life.

"*Beti.*"

We stared at each other, making no move to show any affection. I couldn't remember the last time Papa had hugged me or told me he loved me. It was something I could never expect from him, and I refused to make the first move.

"Come inside." Jacinta broke the standoff. "I have rooms ready for you. You can freshen up before we have dinner and board the riverboat. Dev, will you check on the guests while I get everyone settled in?"

Devin nodded and moved toward the crowd enjoying their cocktails.

I threaded my arm through my mom's and led her toward the steps of the house. Tyler and Ashur joked while Carol and Jacinta engaged my father in a conversation, asking him his opinion of the latest technology trends on the market.

Papa seemed to enjoy the discussion and happily shared his thoughts. Of all my friends, Jacinta had been Papa's favorite. He would go out of his way to make time for her whenever she was around. It was as if he ignored the fact her brother was married to his estranged daughter.

"Mummy," I said in my family's native language of Gujarati.

"Why did Papa come? He can't bear to look at me, much less want to socialize with me."

"Your husband is very persistent."

I gave her the side eye. *"Right. I buy that."* We ascended the steps into the house. *"Mummy, I have to tell you something before you learn about it in the tabloids."*

"I know, sweetheart. You're going to be a politician."

"That's part of it." I paused midstep. *"How do you know this? I haven't made it public."*

"I read the news. All rumors have some truth. Your client likes to talk too much, but he's a smart man and never puts anything out to the public that doesn't have a solid basis. I don't like his tactics but he's never disrespected you. In fact, he adores you."

I wasn't sure what to say. This woman could always pull apart the facts from the fiction.

People assumed I'd inherited my smarts from Papa

with his technology savvy. What most never knew or dared to learn was that Mummy was a child prodigy like I was. She had graduated magna cum laude from Princeton and then by the time she was twenty-three, gained her PhD in computer analytics and physics from Oxford University.

The life she'd planned had taken a dramatic turn when her grandfather arranged her marriage to Papa. She'd cemented her family's place in the Indian community, not by her achievements in science and technology, but by marrying into one of the wealthiest Indian families in the United States.

"Mummy, you are brilliant. No wonder Papa keeps such a tight rein on you. He's afraid you'll overshadow his success."

"Samina—" her voice grew stern, *"—don't go there. Be happy I'm here."*

I released a deep sigh. I'd never win any discussion where it concerned Papa. *"Okay. I hear you."*

"I know you did. Take me to my room." She followed me along the hallway. *"I want to change. Your Papa has a meeting with your father-in-law."*

I frowned as I opened the door to her suite. *"Why?"*

"Business," she responded, and that was the extent of the information she was going to give me.

She had this way of shutting down a subject that left no room for argument. It didn't matter how much I fought with Papa. He never could keep me quiet the way Mummy managed with a glare.

Oh well. I'd better enjoy my time with my mom

instead of worrying about what the two fathers were concocting.

An hour after setting sail from Jacinta's property, I stared at the passing homes along the river. There was so much going on, and I couldn't hide the strain anymore. I'd come to the lower deck, away from the festivities, to refocus and prepare myself for the discussion I'd have with the family after all the guests left.

I could only pretend to enjoy myself for so long. Hell, Jacinta looked exhausted, and she thrived on the chaos of a socialite party. Thankfully, she'd told me about a back passage to this level so that I could escape.

A boom of laughter reached my ears, and I heard the distinct accent and timbre of my father's voice. He was a politician in his own right, using his charisma to charm everyone around him.

Papa still hadn't spoken a full sentence to me. He acted as if I wasn't even in the room, and whenever anyone mentioned my name or asked about my newfound fame, he'd made an underhanded comment like, "That's the life she chose—she can't expect anything less."

I could tell Ashur was doing everything in his willpower to keep from losing his temper every time Papa opened his mouth. During my younger years, I used to resent Ash for being Papa's favorite, but quickly I learned he used his position in the family as a way to keep a buffer between Papa and me.

My big brother dealt with so much crap because of me. I knew he'd have left long ago and told my father to shove his money where the sun didn't shine if I weren't in the picture. Ashur loved me and protected me the way I'd wanted Papa to do.

God, I had such daddy issues.

"Baby, is everything okay?" Devin asked as he sat down next to me. "You barely touched your food at dinner, and you haven't said much since we left the dock. Don't let your father get to you. I heard what he said to Representative Cartwright."

"He wants to hurt me because I didn't follow his plan for my life. And telling others that I didn't have the stomach or will for business is his way of taking a jab at me. It's not as if I was ever going to get to run Kumar Tech. He has strict views on women's roles."

I exhaled and wrung my hands together. He would have done to me what Mummy's family did to her, educate and then marry the prized daughter to the most advantageous alliance. Papa acted modern but was as ass-backward as they got. Hell, most families in India were more open-minded than he was.

There I went again with my daddy angst.

Devin pulled me to his side and pressed my head against his chest.

"I'm glad you didn't say anything to him. I saw your jaw clench," I said as I watched a family jumping into the water from their dock.

"I was tempted, but it would have hurt your election

prospects if I threw my father-in-law off the riverboat. Now tell me what's really bothering you. Are you nervous about the announcement tomorrow?"

I glanced up at him, but he pushed me back against him.

After making love to me in the cabin, Dev and I had touched on my conversation with Tracy but hadn't gone into details. Devin accepted the plan, but something told me he was holding back his true feelings and I was too chicken shit to probe him. What if the loss of his privacy was too much for him? After the pictures came out, we'd become even more of a spectacle.

"Honestly, I'm worried about telling our families about the pictures. The election will be less important to my father than the images of me naked."

"This isn't about him, Sami. Someone illegally took photos of you in a vulnerable state and then threatened to hurt you. If your father can't see your innocence, then he doesn't deserve a single thought. One day Spencer Miller is going to be sorry."

I lifted my face up, and the look in his eyes told me he was planning something.

"What did you do?"

"Ash and I have it under control."

"Excuse me. When did you and my brother become friends again? The last thing I knew, Ash wanted to take you to the gun range and use you for target practice."

"We came to an agreement," Devin said. "Our

differences are secondary to your safety. Plus, your brother missed taking our annual guys' trips."

"I'm not sure if I believe you but I'll buy it for the moment." I pursed my lips and then narrowed my eyes. "Now tell me what the two of you did."

"Let's just say, it helps to have a billion-dollar technology company at our disposal."

I jumped up and paced, pinching the bridge of my nose.

This was bad.

I cocked a hand on my hip. "Devin James Camden, don't do anything to hurt your position. He's not worth it."

I was already about to put him in the spotlight. The last thing I wanted his actions to do was affect his job, or worse, land him in an ethics investigation.

"Stop worrying." He tugged me onto his lap, spreading my legs to straddle him. "Ash is going to use his channels to see if he can buy the pictures before Decker sells them to Sanders."

I gripped his shoulders as his hands slid to my hips. "What if he doesn't budge?"

"Then Ash is going to hack him and wipe the cloud and any electronics the pictures were downloaded onto."

"What?" I jerked; however, he held on to me so I couldn't stand. "When did you have time to plan this? I know it couldn't have been between fucking me four times today and mingling with potential donors."

"I called him after our date the other night. I will break

every law to make sure some scumbag doesn't terrorize my wife."

"Okay, Mr. Rule-and-law-breaker. What have you done with my do-everything-by-the-book husband and when can I get him back?"

"Very funny." He cupped the back of my head. "I will do what is necessary."

"I'm serious. Devin, let me handle this. I have a plan. I'm not going to let any man dictate my future ever again. Even you."

He glowered at me, but before he could respond, Jacinta and Ashur rushed toward us.

"Do you two do anything other than fuck?" Jacinta pulled me off Devin then handed me her phone. "We have a crisis. Talk to him."

"Hello."

"Sam, darlin'. If you don't get ahead of this, we're up shit creek." Clint Bassett's voice surprised me.

"Umm. Clint. Why are you calling me on Jacinta's line?"

"Because I couldn't get hold of you."

"What's going on?"

"Someone named Spencer Miller offered me compromising pictures of you in exchange for a spot on my show."

A lump formed in the pit of my stomach, and I looked up at Jacinta. She clenched her fists and shook her head. Ash was no better. Then I glanced at Devin who was reading something on his phone. He ran a frustrated hand through his hair.

"Did you take the offer?" My voice cracked.

"For the love of all that is good, I would never shit on you like that. I told that fucker to jump off the nearest cliff."

"Thank you."

"What are you thanking me for? Girl, I know what you've been planning, and I'm going to get you elected. Do you hear me? Why do you think I did all the things to put you in the spotlight? You needed a platform, and I gave it to you."

I leaned against the railing of the boat and let the breeze cool the July heat from my body.

"Clint, who has the pictures? I know you know."

He remained quiet for a second and then spoke. "The photographs went out ten minutes ago to all the major gossip sites. The fucker mentioned Sanders would pay me handsomely to release them on all my social media platforms."

"You wouldn't happen to have recorded that?"

"You know me well. Yes, I have that asshat recorded. Miller also had Sanders on the line during the conversation. The dipshit thinks I'm some idiot who doesn't understand how these things are played. There is no way that fucker Sanders can pretend Miller did this on his own."

"Will you send it to me? No, send it to Tracy. I know she's the one who leaked my plans to you."

I peeked over my shoulder and saw Devin watching me intently. A frown marred his beautiful face as well as worry. I wanted to reassure him, but it would be a lie. This was a new game, and I was a pawn. Well, at least that's what Sanders believed.

"I'm tempted to release the tape. That would show Sanders's loyal supporters what a shithead he is. I'm sorry for the language, Sam. I just can't stand men like this using their power to hurt the women who challenge them. I have four daughters, for Christ's sake."

I couldn't help but smile. The shock jock was outraged at the injustice of my situation.

"Clint," I said, taking a deep breath, "I am going to handle this my way. If you want to help me, wait until I make my announcement. Do not do anything that will take away from the press conference I am going to have tomorrow morning."

"You better make it good."

"Clint, I mean it. Don't fuck this up by opening your mouth."

He chuckled. "Yes, ma'am. That's the bossy lady I first met. I take it your husband has fixed things with you."

"Clint," I warned, making him laugh harder in response.

"Good. I'd hate to have to kick his ass. Now, go show those bastards who's in charge."

"I'll do my best." I hung up and handed Jacinta the phone.

She snatched it out of my hand. "Care to fill me in or should I guess?"

Ashur walked up and sat next to Dev, who hadn't moved the whole time I was on the phone. "So, it's a go?"

"What's a go?" Jacinta asked.

"Dev and Ash, don't for one minute think to take over. Do I make myself clear?" I stood and then began to pace. "I love both of you, but this is my battle."

Jacinta waved her hand. "Hello. Someone get me up to speed or I'm going to lose it."

"Spencer Miller released the pictures." Dev stared into my eyes. "And my wife is going to counter by announcing her candidacy."

CHAPTER SEVENTEEN

"I need someone to stop and tell me when I entered the Twilight Zone," Jacinta demanded.

Dev stared at me. "You heard me. My wife is going to give you the highlight of the holiday weekend. She will announce her bid for Senate in the morning."

"Something tells me I shouldn't get too excited. So, spill it." Her eyes flashed at me, giving me her "you better start talking" look.

I approached Jacinta, taking her hand in mine.

"I don't know how to tell you this."

"Just say it, Sam."

I peered into her eyes, knowing my words would bring back memories she'd done so much to overcome.

"Decker arranged for Sanders to acquire the pictures. They are going to use them to discredit all of us."

She flinched but kept her face emotionless. "I'm sorry, Sam. It's my fault."

"The hell it is!" I shouted. "I am convenient. I'm an easy target."

Her voice was cold when she spoke again. "I was the one who started this. I am challenging Decker for his job. He knows I've made it my life's mission to get rid of men like him and his son."

I looked over Jacinta's shoulder to find Dev and Ashur watching us with deep scrutiny, telling me I was going to have to do some explaining.

Hopefully, both of them would understand I'd made a promise to keep Jacinta's shame a secret.

"Jaci, he can't hurt you anymore. I had every piece of evidence wiped. I know people like to say there is always a trace. There is none. I even had people sweep each property for physical evidence."

The one and only time I'd ever used my connections in the tech world was to have some of the top hackers in the world break into Decker Senior's and Junior's systems and destroy any and all records of Jacinta.

"You did what?" Ashur asked. "Sam, you are running for Congress. You can't go invading people's private files."

"You don't know why I did it."

"Then explain it to me." He moved to the railing and glowered at me.

Shit, my big brother was going to hand me my ass when we were alone.

I crossed my arms over my chest. "It's not my story to tell. Just know I wouldn't hesitate to do it again. Like what you and Devin were planning to do to help me, I did what I needed to protect those I love. But unlike you, I had Jacinta's permission to protect her."

"Samina, what if you were caught?"

"Ash, seriously? I knew what I was doing. You aren't the only one who knows how to tinker with computers. I've always had the tech skills you and Papa possess. Law was Papa's choice for my life, not mine."

Jacinta squeezed my hand.

"Jaci," Devin said in a soft whisper. "Come sit with me."

He opened his arms, and a single tear fell from Jacinta's eye as she moved to the bench and into Devin's embrace.

"I don't need the story, little bean." My heart melted hearing him use the nickname he'd called her when she was little. "When did he do it?"

As she rested her head on his shoulder, she said, "Five years ago. That weekend Dad sent me as his representative to the PAC gala."

I still remembered getting her call. I'd dropped everything to fly to her and then bring her to Seattle. At the time, Devin was on the campaign trail with his father and wasn't around to ask questions.

"Did you hurt him?"

God, I loved this man. He knew Jacinta hated anyone thinking she was weak, and his question kept her from falling apart. The last thing she'd want was someone's pity.

"Yes, he went to the hospital." She gave a halfhearted smirk. "I broke his nose and cracked his ribs. I guess I learned a few things in the MMA classes Sam forced me to attend twice a week for three years."

Devin's eyes burned with a sense of sadness that broke my heart. I knew he felt like he'd failed his sister and me.

"Jaci, I'm going to expose Decker and what he did to me. I'll keep your name out of it, but I'm going to fight, even if it costs me the election," I said, taking a seat next to her.

"No, Sam. He's going to help Sanders ruin not only your reputation but your career. Thanks to you, he has nothing on me anymore. I am the darling of my party. I represent the future my party is desperate to push to the forefront. The only way to get to me is through you."

"I'm a trust-fund kid. I don't ever have to work. Besides, your brother can be my sugar daddy for a change."

My joke fell flat, and she blew out a frustrated breath. "Samina."

"Don't Samina me. I know what I'm doing. This situation won't be the last time a bastard like him will try to hurt us. Your father is right. This is life for women in politics. I'm not going anywhere so I'll have to get used to it." I stared into Jacinta's eyes. "I love you, Jaci. But I refuse to pretend it didn't happen, and what Miller did to me isn't anywhere near what you and countless other women experienced."

She remained quiet, but the pain etched on her face told me I'd hit the mark. I hated hurting her. She was my best friend, my sister. I wished to God she'd pressed charges, but she hadn't and the asshole had gone free. At least karma caught up to him and the fucker was now dealing with the consequences of a high-profile drug arrest.

"You are so strong, Jaci. And I understand what it cost you to stay silent for your dad's and Tyler's sakes. I'm going to stand up to Decker and Sanders for me and for every woman like you who had to remain quiet, who had to pretend nothing happened to her in order to protect others or who were shamed into stepping aside."

She was quiet for a few minutes thinking, then linked her fingers with mine.

"I'm going to have to reveal what he did and why he's helping Sanders." Jacinta said it as a statement, not a question.

"That's up to you. Clint has Sanders recorded when he thought Miller was on hold. We can't use the recording in a criminal investigation, but I'm sure Clint would leak the content of the conversation. We can keep any mention of what Decker's son did to you out of the media."

"Let me think about it. I need to talk to my campaign manager before I disclose anything that happened to me."

I nodded. "Okay. I'll support you, no matter what you decide. But we have to get anyone involved with our campaigns up to date, including Veer, since he has ties to both of us."

"Sam, promise me you won't tell Veer what happened yet."

"Why not?"

"Because he will kill Decker. They've hated each other since the comments he made questioning Veer's service in the military. This election is too important. Veer has to win."

"I'll win whether I punch Decker Senior or not." Veer stood in the doorway leading onto the deck.

Jacinta stiffened. "How long have you been there?"

"Long enough." He stared at Jacinta and me. "Carol asked me to find you before the fireworks started."

"Do you want me to fill you in?" I asked, trying to move his attention from Jacinta to me.

"No." He pulled out his phone. "I was notified a few minutes ago."

My heart dropped. How was I going to face Mummy?

"Does anyone else know?"

"I doubt it. Our families and the guests are preparing for the show. Your former client sent me a message. He wanted to have me on hand when 'the shit hit the fan.' Those are his words, not mine."

"Trust Clint to put things in perspective." I studied Jacinta. "You okay?"

She had her head back and eyes closed, her telltale sign she had a raging migraine.

Veer walked up to us and stretched out his hand. "Let's go, Ms. Camden. We'll get you something for your headache and then you can explain the conversation I walked in on."

Without protesting as I'd expected whenever someone

bossed her about, she stood and slid her palm over Veer's. They left without a backward glance.

Dev cleared his throat, bringing my attention to him, and then lifted a brow.

I shrugged my shoulders and then said, "Don't ask me. I have no idea what that's about. I was only kidding about them when I made the comment at the house."

Ashur pushed me toward Dev and then sat beside me. "So, little sis, I guess you're going to announce tomorrow."

"Yep."

"How do you feel about it?" He leaned over and smirked at Devin.

"I like my privacy, but I love her. There's no contest. I'm with her all the way." Devin picked up my hand, kissing my fingers.

"This puts our plans on hold. The dirt is now public. I'd still like to put a virus on Decker's, Sanders's, and Miller's systems."

"Not happening. I'm going to have enough trouble without you two adding to it," I informed my brother. "You should be thanking me for keeping you from doing anything that hedged the law."

"What we planned wasn't hedging, it was full-on illegal."

I stared at Devin as if he'd lost his mind. "How can you be so casual and nonchalant about breaking the law?" Then I glared at Ashur. "You too, Mr. War Hero and Defender of Those Who Were Wronged."

"It's not like I'm running for president. When have I cared about image or what others thought of me?"

Ash was known for speaking his mind, never worrying if someone agreed with him or not. He also had this ability to insult someone to their face without them realizing it.

"Point taken. If you had the stomach to handle the nonstop socializing and ass-kissing, you'd be the one running. I guess you'll have to leave it to those of us with the stamina."

"Hey, squirt. Did you just insult me?" Ash pinched my shoulder.

"You should know. You're the master of the subtle insult," Devin interjected, resulting in me giving him a fist-bump and then laughing.

"Who's going to run the campaign? You need someone with a straight head on their shoulders and the fortitude to handle the chaos."

"Ash, are you volunteering for the job? That would require you to move to Seattle."

"Not happening. I cannot ever have you as a boss. You'd make my life a living hell. Although, the idea of living near you is tolerable."

I elbowed him. "Good save."

"There's only one choice," Devin said. "Tara Zain. She is brilliant, organized, and takes no one's bullshit."

Ashur remained quiet but I saw him stare into the distance.

"You still haven't forgiven her, have you?"

"I got over it a long time ago."

"For the record, she loved you."

"That's not how I saw it. Tara dropped me the second she found out she got accepted to Harvard. She was looking for a bigger fish."

I shoved Ashur. "She isn't like that, and I resent you implying something so stupid."

"Then pray tell me why she broke up with me."

"Papa forced her to end it with you or her parents would lose their jobs. She loved you, but her family isn't from the same economic or social standing as ours. Why do you think they moved to Washington? It was a place where Papa had no reach."

He was quiet, lost in thought for a few seconds, then he shook his head.

"It isn't important anymore. I'm over it. All that matters is that you have someone competent to head your campaign."

I smirked. "Yes, that was so convincing."

"Shut it, squirt."

"Stop calling me that. Squirt is what you call a ten-year-old kid. I'm a grown woman about to run for Senate."

"I can attest to the grown woman part," Dev interjected. "I've studied every part of her in great detail."

Ashur groaned. "I thought you were a conservative judge with strict morals. Why is sex the only thing on your mind?"

"Because your sister puts out in the best way possible."

"Dev, man. Do you have to go there? I think I threw up a little in my mouth."

This was fabulous. After all these years, Dev and Ash were friends again and back to the back-and-forth banter I remembered from long ago.

All of a sudden, I felt a wave of nausea and anxiety, and my joy evaporated as did that of the men next to me.

We remained silent for a few minutes, taking in the night before I spoke.

"We're not going to be able to do this for a long time. Are we?"

"It comes with the territory. In a few hours, even the little bit of privacy you've managed to enjoy will disappear."

"I know, Ash. They're going to be on everyone, you included."

"I'm an asshole so no one will bother me. I'll just growl in their direction and the media will scatter."

"Thank you." I took hold of each of their hands. "I love you both so much."

"We love you too."

"Speak for yourself," Dev said as he ran a thumb along the vein on the outside of my hand. "I know for a fact I love her in a different way than you do. One that is much more intimate."

"Devin! Really? She's my sister."

I rolled my eyes. Seeing this goofy and a bit pervy side of Dev was always fun.

"You both are crazy." I stood. "Let's go and pretend to

enjoy ourselves for the next hour. As soon as we dock, all hell is going to break loose."

Before I finished my statement, a set of lights flashed on and a helicopter descended toward the boat.

Devin jumped up, shoving me behind him.

"I think it already did."

CHAPTER EIGHTEEN

"Let's go, Sami. We have to get you inside. The crowd along the border of the compound has tripled." Devin wrapped his arm around my waist as we ran toward Jacinta's house.

The second the helicopter lights had flashed on, I knew the media would be camped out in full force. Ashur and Veer had called in friends of theirs who specialized in high-profile client security. The team mobilized within twenty minutes and were doing an incredible job of keeping anyone and everyone away from the house.

I couldn't help but feel bad for all the guests in the boat that had to cut their evening short. All of Jacinta's Independence Day festivities had gone down the toilet. There had been a lot of confusion and rumors as the boat emptied. Thankfully, Jacinta had arranged for transportation to be waiting for everyone to leave.

I entered the kitchen and headed straight for the fridge, pulling out a bottle of sparkling water and drinking deep.

My stomach was in knots, and I had to settle it before I faced my parents.

Resting my hand on my abdomen, I closed my eyes.

"Are you ready?"

I shook my head and said, "Give me a few more minutes."

"Baby, you can't hide in the kitchen. Our families are waiting for us."

I looked up at him. "Dev, this is only the beginning. Are you sure you can handle this?"

"Yes. I'm prepared." He gripped the edge of the island.

"I mean it. I'm making my announcement in a few hours. Once I do this, there is no going back. If you have any doubts, tell me now."

"When are you going to understand I'm here for good? What do I have to do to prove I'm committed?" He clenched his jaw. "I know I fucked up. But you can't keep expecting me to let you down."

Before I could argue, Veer walked in. "Sorry to interrupt but the parents are beginning to circle. Everyone is in the family room. I'd get the discussion over with as soon as possible. You have enough on your plate."

Nodding, I took another sip from the bottle.

I released a deep breath, set my water on the counter, and made my way past Devin and Veer.

I walked down the hallway and opened the door to find both dads pacing, the moms pretending to sip drinks, and Tyler, Jacinta, and Ashur on their phones.

Veer moved into the room, positioned himself by the window next to Ashur, and pulled out his own mobile.

"Samina, I want an explanation this minute. What is this spectacle outside? How could you let someone take pictures of you?" Papa demanded in Gujarati. *"Do you have any idea what this will do to our reputation, to the company stock? Have you no integrity?"*

"Let her talk," Mummy pleaded. *"She didn't take the pictures. How can you blame her?"*

"Anya, stay out of this. She is turning our family name into a laughingstock."

Ashur stuffed his phone into his pants pocket and responded in English. "Leave her alone, Papa. Mummy only speaks the truth."

Papa loved to use our language when it kept others from knowing what he was saying. This was his not-so-subtle way of making the Camdens feel excluded. Ashur responding in English made it look like he was challenging Papa.

Papa narrowed his eyes. "I am still the head of this family. If you don't like the way I do things, get out."

Ashur opened his mouth to respond but stopped when he saw me shake my head. It was time to stand up to the man who thought of me as a commodity instead of a child.

I approached my father. "Papa, what happened was an act of a coward. He broke into my house and took pictures of me in the shower, and then threatened to hurt me. I was lucky to get away from him before he was able to lay a hand on me."

"You invited this kind of act. If you hadn't let him—" he glowered at Devin, "—or that Zain girl influence you, you'd be married to a respectable man and in a respectable position. Not become this trash magazine starlet." He gestured to me as a whole.

"Papa," Ash warned, "tread carefully."

"Samina, you are an embarrassment. How could you throw away everything I've done for you to live a life like this?"

He made it sound as if I were a whore who fucked anyone who asked. He was like all those who blame the victims of a crime.

Devin's palm slid around my waist, giving me the grounding I needed to stand up to Papa.

"What you can't handle is that I made a success of my life without a penny from you."

"Do you think your education came for free?"

Papa tried to tower his six-foot height over me, but Devin shifted me to his side.

"I know who paid for my college and law school, and it wasn't you. Mummy's trust fund paid every dime of it. Did you think I didn't know you'd have married me to the most advantageous bidder?" I pinched the bridge of my nose. "Indians in India aren't as back-assed backward as you are. Hell, most of the *Desi* girls I know have fathers who would do anything to support their daughters' dreams."

"You disgraced us by breaking with tradition. Do you know what kind of life you would have had if only you'd listened? Everything was at your fingertips."

"You mean if I'd let you control me as you'd done my whole life."

"Don't put words in my mouth. This is your last warning, Samina. Show some respect, or there will be consequences."

His words triggered all the men in the room to shift, readying to step between us. Even Richard was shocked by the threat and positioned himself next to Veer at an angle to grab hold of Papa.

"I'm not a child anymore, Papa. I don't owe you anything. I am a successful litigator with a thriving practice. So what if my clients don't meet your standards. You've never met mine. Now if you'll excuse me. I'll be writing my speech to announce my candidacy for the Senate."

I whirled around, turning my back to my father. He would never accept me, and I was done trying.

Before I could take a step, he grabbed me by the arm. "Over my dead body will you sell yourself as a politician."

"Let her go," Devin ordered. "Or I will take great pleasure in breaking every one of your fingers."

Papa released his hold, shooting daggers at me with his eyes. "I can't believe you'd whore yourself for the ambitions of this family."

"Now wait just a minute." Richard moved toward

Papa. "You will not disrespect my family by insulting what we do to make our nation great."

"Great? You sell yourself to the highest donor." Papa stared me down. "Samina, if you enter this election, you will never be welcome in my home again."

"How is that different than now? I haven't been home in five years," I countered. "You disgust me. You are no better than the bullies who I'm going to fight. At least Richard has the decency to try to make a difference. You sit on your high horse, rolling in your money. Never once have you thought to use it for good."

"Don't you lecture me. I'm your father."

"Then act like it."

His eyes narrowed. "You want to challenge me? I've put up with you marrying someone who didn't fit into our culture. I put up with your sensationalist career. If for one damn minute you think I won't put all my money behind your opponent to keep you out of office then you have another think coming."

I swayed. Papa would destroy me to make a point.

"Enough," Ashur voiced as he stepped next to me. "Papa, this conversation is done. You will never threaten my sister or anyone again. As of this day, you no longer have a son. Everyone knows you don't have a daughter."

Papa snorted. "Say that when the money runs out. Who's going to pay for all your charity projects? Are you going to leave all your fellow veterans without funding?"

"We don't need your money. I've always known how you felt about my military service and the charities I started." Ashur took my hand. "You've spent so much time worrying about your image to notice what was happening in your company. I haven't taken a salary in years. The money I spend is from real estate deals I made using the revenue I earned selling Bitcoin before the bust."

"You ungrateful pissant. Both of you have made your choice. Don't come crawling back to me when you fall flat on your asses." Papa turned to Mummy. "Get up. We're leaving."

Mummy stayed where she was.

"Anya, I said get up." He walked over to her and bellowed, "Now."

She remained still, not flinching an inch. After years of this, she never showed any outward reaction to Papa's outbursts. She straightened the pleats on her dress, took a shaky breath, and then said, "I'm staying with my children."

"So that's how it is?"

"Yes." She lifted her chin. "You would hurt my babies, destroy everything they've worked for as a way to control them. I can't stand by any longer. To my regret, I kept quiet when you threw our daughter out of our home. I should have said something long ago, especially after Devin begged you to be part of their lives. My baby married without me because of you. It ends now. I will not watch her have children from a distance. Devin is a better man than you'll ever be."

"How is he better? He kept her a secret. He went out with other women. She went out with other men. He lived with her like a kept woman. Do you think others didn't know he was ashamed of her? If he loved her so much and was so much better than me, why did he hide her from his parents? She was his Indian whore, nothing more."

My heart sank, and all the pain I'd worked to try and push back resurfaced. Papa was right. Devin had done everything he said. But what Papa couldn't understand was that I was just as responsible for accepting the relationship I was in.

God, I wanted my mom to leave my father, and I'd stayed in just as shitty a marriage.

My eyes filled and tears spilled down my cheeks.

Devin squeezed my waist and then whispered into my hair, "I'm so sorry, baby. Forgive me."

Then before I could respond to him, he turned and walked out the door. I wanted to follow him, to demand why he left.

"See, I'm right. That boy can't face the truth. That's why he ran away. Samina, you will forget this boy, forget this election, and come home."

I clenched my fists. Papa was not going to win. He'd ruled so much of my life, even after I'd married and moved to Seattle.

"No. I'll never return. Washington is my home. No matter what happens with my marriage, I will continue to live there."

I scanned the faces of my mom, Ashur, Veer, Carol, Tyler, and Jacinta. They were my family. They truly loved and cared for me without conditions.

I tilted my chin up. "I love him. And no matter what you say, I will fight for my marriage until there is no hope."

"What hope? Did you not hear a word of what I said?" Papa shook his head like I was some stupid girl.

"She heard you." Richard came to stand by me and put his hand on my shoulder. "We all did. Samina deserves better. From all of us, especially you. What kind of father says and does the things you've done?"

"Don't give me your sanctimonious bullshit."

"Stop it now." Carol rose, cocking a hand on her hip and pointing to the door. "It is time you left. And remember this, if you cause anyone in my family trouble, I will make sure you regret it. You're not the only one with money or connections."

Until that moment, I'd forgotten Carol was an heir to an oil fortune. She probably had more weight to her requests than Papa could ever dream of possessing.

"Are you threatening me?" Papa challenged.

"Yes," Mummy answered, coming to my other side and slipping her hand into mine. "My money started your empire. I'm still majority stockholder. Don't act so surprised. I know everything that goes on in the company. You hurt either of my children, I will fire you from the company you love more than your family."

Okay, what was happening? Mummy and Carol were standing up to Papa without fear of repercussion.

God, I loved these women.

I had to stop this from getting worse. We all had enough to handle with the press outside.

"Papa, please."

He ignored me and moved to the door. "You've made your choices."

Without another word, he opened the door and walked out of the room.

CHAPTER NINETEEN

"Shorty, let's finish this so I can head home and get some sleep," Veer said as he pulled me into the library to work on my announcement.

It had taken over an hour to handle the aftermath of my father's departure. I was on the verge of collapse and shaking from exhaustion.

I hadn't seen any sign of Devin since he left in the middle of the argument, and when I'd asked about him, Ashur informed me that Devin was handling media outlets who were contacting everyone we knew.

I guess it was a good thing I hadn't seen him. I wasn't sure what I was going to say when we had a moment alone.

Papa's words echoed in my mind, and I couldn't get over the hurt and memories they brought up.

Why did I let my father get to me so much?

Mummy insisted he loved me, but Papa's form of love was overbearing and controlling.

For such a smart man, he was an idiot who couldn't see that his actions had now lost his relationship with both his children. My jaw clenched thinking of the jabs he'd made toward Ashur.

What more did Papa want from him? Most parents would think of him as the jackpot in the parenting lottery. Who didn't want a child who was a war hero and had created a billion-dollar fortune on his own merit?

Tears prickled my eyes.

"Sam, have you heard a word I said?"

I shook the fog from my mind and focused on Veer. "Sorry. Say it one more time."

He released an exasperated sigh. "Stop worrying about your father. You have too much to focus on to let him dictate your life and your decisions anymore."

"What the hell are you talking about, Veer?"

"Your father uses his money as a way to control people, but with you he uses manipulation."

I rested both of my hands against the back of a chair in the corner of the library as I glared at Veer. "I'm not weak minded. I told him to go fuck himself years ago and then I did it again today."

He walked up to me and shook his head. "You still haven't admitted it to yourself, have you?"

"Veer, my head hurts, I'm drained both emotionally and physically, and now I have to figure out what the fuck I'm going to say tomorrow. I don't need you psychoanalyzing me."

Why wouldn't he let this drop?

"Pretending isn't going to change the fact that it's true."

I clenched my teeth and thought about punching him. I couldn't care less that he was a good foot and some change taller than me.

"Fine, tell me, Mr. Knows-Everything. What have I not admitted?"

"That because of Minesh Kumar, you stayed in a marriage that was destroying you from the inside out."

I touched my chest and closed my eyes for a moment. "Dev's making an effort to change. Hell, look what he did to get my parents here. I can't imagine what Papa must have said to him."

Papa used the crudest language when the public wasn't watching. The way he'd spoken tonight was barely the tip of things he was capable of voicing.

"I'm happy you're working it out, but that doesn't change the truth of what I said."

"Let it go, Veer."

"You're the attorney. Would you let it go?"

"You're such a pain in the ass."

"Give me something to make sense of it all. Samina, you are a catch any man should be honored to have. Why did you stay with Devin all these years? And don't say love. I know it's bullshit and you do too."

"You don't know anything, Veer Kiran George. Devin Camden is the only man I love and will ever love."

"That's not the reason you refused to leave him. No matter how much Ash and I tried to convince you to come back to Texas, you stayed. Hell, your best friend, his sister, wanted you to leave his ass."

I folded my arms across my body. I couldn't deny Veer's claims.

"No woman with your education, career, or money puts up with the way you were treated unless there is a reason. I know the reason, Ash knows the reason, and sure as hell, your father knows the reason. I even suspect Devin knows the reason. Why can't you admit the truth?"

"Fine. You want to know why I stayed. I stayed because..." I paused as the door to the library was pushed open.

"I'd like an answer to that question as well."

"Dev," I whispered.

He peered at me and repeated his previous statement. "Finish what you were going to say to Veer. I'd like the answer to his question, as well."

I looked between Veer and Devin, my heart beating out of my chest.

Veer walked up to me and kissed my cheek. "Tell him, little sis. He deserves to know. Maybe it will help you admit it to yourself too. And then you can truly start fresh as a couple."

Veer turned, walking past Devin and shutting the door behind him.

We remained quiet for a few seconds, gazing at each other before I walked onto the balcony.

I stared toward the river and rubbed my arms as a chill

shot through me even though it was at least a hundred Fahrenheit.

This was a conversation that was years in the making, one we'd touched on here and there but never addressed.

Devin approached me, leaning against the balcony railing next to me.

"If not for love, tell me why you stayed." Pain laced his words. The truth was going to hurt him as much as it hurt me to admit it.

"Because...because I refused to let my father win. I wasn't going to fail at my marriage as he predicted. He told me we'd never last. He said you didn't understand me or what my dreams were. That you couldn't care less about our culture and would push me to turn my back on it, instead of trying to become part of it. He insisted you only cared about your career and your family's reputation. He predicted our love wouldn't survive your ambition or mine." I turned toward him. "I loved you so much, but I'd never have allowed the way things went with us if I wasn't determined to prove him wrong. I tolerated a marriage like my parents', all because I was never going to let Papa see that he was, in fact, right."

He stepped toward me, grasping my upper arms with both of his hands. "But he's not right. Don't let his words change the road we're trying to mend. We can fix this. I won't ever take you for granted again."

Why was he so calm? I'd just told him I stayed in our marriage because of Papa and not him.

"Why aren't you angry about what I've just admitted?"

"I already knew why you held on for so long." He released me and then ran a frustrated hand through his hair. "I've known since we started having problems."

I remembered the first time I realized our marriage was in trouble. Devin had been angry with me that morning two years ago. I'd taken on a new client who happened to be the wife of a major critic of his father's. He'd left my condo after a heated argument about loyalties and then returned, threw a stack of papers on the coffee table, and said he was now officially a nominee for federal magistrate judge.

I hadn't spoken to him for over a month. We lived in the same condo, neither acknowledging the other's presence. The only way we ever expressed ourselves was in bed every night through angry sex, filled with pain, need.

It was a repeated cycle we visited every time things became complicated.

"That was years ago."

"You should have left me then. Hell, you should have left me before that. But you stayed. You put up with my crap, no matter how much it hurt."

"Like when you took that bitch Veronica to all your family events or Judge McGregor to the charity event."

"Yes." He hung his head. "I was such a bastard. It won't ever happen again. It should have been you by my side from the beginning."

"There's so much hurt between us. Is it possible to move past it? Is a fresh start going to work or are we kidding ourselves?" Tears streamed down my face as I peered up at him. "I won't be the woman who let you turn her into a secret anymore. As I told you in Seattle, I'd rather live without you and have a broken heart than with you and be less than who I am."

"I'll do whatever it takes to make this work. We made a vow on that beach. To love, honor, and cherish each other through thick or thin. Don't give up on us. I won't ever let you down."

"Our lives are going to become insane. I'm going to fight Sanders and Decker. It's going to get dirty. After what happened tonight with Papa, I have to do this for all those who've encountered someone who used their power to hurt them." I closed my eyes, letting my tears fall. "So please don't make promises if you can't keep them."

"You're more important to me than anything. When the time comes, I'll take an indefinite leave of absence and be by your side every step of the way."

I couldn't believe what he said. He was going to put his career aside for me. He loved his position. It was all he'd ever wanted. I knew what he'd told his father, but I hadn't thought he'd stop working.

"That's not something I'd ask of you."

"I know you wouldn't. I'm making the choice. I'm all in, baby. Now the ball is in your court. You decide how things go for us. I'm not going to say things will be easy. My parents' marriage is proof enough, but as long as we agree to meet each other halfway, we can survive anything thrown our way."

I held his gaze, seeing the truth in his words. What he'd been trying to tell me since he muscled his way back into our house. All these years we'd let other people dictate our actions. It was time to live honestly. The way we should have from the beginning.

I had to trust this, trust him. I either forgave the past and moved forward, or I had to give him up.

"I'm in, Sami. Are you?"

After a few more seconds, I nodded. "I'm in too."

Relief played across his face, and he pulled me toward him. I buried my face in his chest, feeling the first wave of sadness evaporate from my shoulders.

"What about your father?"

"What about him? He has no say in what I do."

I pulled back. "He's going to go ballistic. Your mom told me he's hoping you'll change your mind about a judicial nomination by the president."

"That's my father's plan for my life, not mine. It's time your career took priority over mine."

I pointed toward the vans and media outlets on the edge of the estate. "Are you ready for that on a regular basis? Once we go down this path, it will be a long time before we become private citizens again."

"I've never been a private citizen. Did you forget my father is a career politician? And you have groupies because of our dear friend Clint. Your privacy went out the window months ago, with no return in sight. Though his need to protect you has started to win me over."

"I'm sure he will be happy to hear about your change in esteem."

"I'll deny it if you ever tell him, but I think he is going to be one of your biggest assets."

"I'll keep it between us."

"I have a request."

"Go ahead." I lifted a brow and then folded my arms.

He caged me against the balcony. "If I stop judicial duties, I have one condition."

Of course he did.

"And what would that be?" I asked, smiling up at him.

He was so handsome.

"A baby." He traced my bottom lip with his thumb. "If I'm quitting my job, I'd like to be upgraded to stay-at-home dad."

My lips trembled. I'd wanted a baby for so long, and until this moment, it never felt like the right time.

"Are you sure you want a baby now? Elections and pregnancy might not be a good combination."

His face broke out into a huge smile. "I don't think you have a choice in the matter."

"Of course I have a choice. I'm the one who has to carry our child." I leaned against the railing and frowned.

"What's today's date?"

"Well, it's past midnight, so July fifth. What does that have to do with any..." I trailed off as I realized where he was going with his question.

The last time I had had a period was almost two months ago. How could I not notice until now? I'd had a period on the first or second of the month like clockwork since I was a teenager. Then when I went on the pill, I could predict it to the hour.

The exhaustion and crying weren't just because of the case or the separation.

Holy shit. I was pregnant.

CHAPTER TWENTY

A wave of dizziness flooded my head, making my stomach turn.

"Oh God. I think I need to sit down."

Before I knew what was happening, Dev scooped me up and carried me through the balcony doors toward the sofa in the middle of the library.

He sat me down and walked over to a hidden cabinet housing a refrigerator. He pulled out a bottle of sparkling water and brought it back, unscrewing the cap and handing it to me.

"Drink. It will settle your stomach."

I followed his directions and then leaned my head back against the couch. I went through every possibility over the last few months, and the only conclusion was that one fateful evening a little over six weeks ago.

"The beach."

"Yes, the beach," he said as he sat next to me.

"When did you figure it out?"

He propped his arm on the back of the sofa, rested a hand on my stomach, and began to draw circles.

"I started to have my suspicions when you kept refusing your favorite drinks, but blew them off, thinking you wanted to keep a level head and not risk the challenge of the alcohol content of Jacinta's concoctions. Then, at dinner, your face turned green as you smelled the steak on your plate. You love a seared tenderloin."

"So, my aversion to red meat confirmed your virility?"

"Yes. And the fact I've been inside your body multiple times a day since the first of this month."

"Oh."

"Why didn't you tell me you'd stopped taking birth control?"

"I didn't." I faced him. "This wasn't planned. I missed a pill here and there over the last few months and thought nothing about it. You couldn't look at me, much less want to screw my brains out. What happened six weeks ago was unexpected."

"For the record, I always want to screw your brains out."

I glared at him. "Devin. Really?"

"That night, I watched you sleep on the lounger for over thirty minutes. Then you moaned my name, and it was all over. I had to have you."

"If I recall, you had me five times. I could barely walk the next morning."

He smiled, but it didn't reach his eyes. "I wish I'd said

to you the words I'd planned. The reason why I came to see you in the first place.

"Instead of talking to you, I made love to you and then lost it when Clint called to discuss the case and the paparazzi showed up. It went from me begging you to take me back to me giving you an ultimatum to pick between our relationship and your career."

"It wasn't one of your better moments. If you want to know the truth, your words that night were the catalyst for me wanting to file for separation. It pushed me to realize that I had to put myself first for a change, no matter what anyone thought."

"However devastated I was to get the notice, I knew I deserved it." He cupped my face and ran a thumb over my lower lip. "I destroyed the most important thing I had in my life for over twelve years. My relationship with you."

I covered his hand with mine. "I'm as much to blame, if not more. I allowed this to happen."

"I did learn some interesting news last week after you made me leave our property."

"I did not make you leave. No one can make you do anything. Case in point, you muscled your way back into the house on the first. Now tell me what you discovered, super sleuth."

"I discovered we aren't separated. You never filed the paperwork."

I cringed. I'd forgotten in all the chaos of the past few days to mention the fact.

"Are you mad?"

"No. Although, you had me convinced."

"How did you find out?"

"I was searching the records for the exact date you filed so I could figure out what day you decided it was over. You have no idea how happy I was to find nothing and to know you hadn't given up hope."

"I'm a sucker for you, Judge Camden."

"Sami." He lifted my chin. "I want us to do things right this time. We can't keep going around in circles taking the same actions and expect different results. We can't brush our problems under the rug like we tend to do."

"And pretend to fix it through sex," I added.

"As much as I hate to agree, you're right. Sex is our way to cover up the real problems. Now, I'm not saying give up sex altogether, I'm saying we have to address whatever issues we're having before falling into bed." He sat back, pulling me against him. "Agreed?"

"Agreed." I closed my eyes, listening to his heart beating a slow, steady rhythm.

Now we had to tell our families. Carol and Mummy were going to be ecstatic, but I wasn't sure how Richard would react. He'd supported me against Papa, but that didn't mean he'd turned over a new leaf on his traditional views of politics.

"Stop worrying about them. This is the first time in our lives that our parents' expectations have no influence on us."

I turned my head up toward him. "Then kiss me and keep me from thinking."

"I thought you said no sex."

"I said no sex to solve our problems. Kissing is not sex."

He sat up, pushing me onto my back, and hovered over me. He leaned down as I lifted my face, but he bypassed my lips and grazed my cheek with his nose. Then he trailed down my neck.

"What are you doing? I said I wanted a kiss."

I grabbed his face and tried to urge him to my lips, but he grasped my wrists in a tight hold, pinning them to the couch.

"You requested a kiss. What you didn't do was specify where. Hold on to the armrest and don't move those hands."

My heartbeat accelerated, and my skin tingled. Wetness pooled between my legs as my nipples stiffened into hard peaks.

"I did not hear a protest, so I take it you like where I want to kiss you."

"Devin," I whimpered.

Who wouldn't want his talented mouth on them?

He cupped my breasts through my dress, pinching the tips, and then moved lower, gathering the hem of my maxi dress. He pushed my legs apart and wedged his shoulder in between.

He leaned down toward my exposed underwear and then stared up at me with a wicked grin.

"This is for my eyes only. All I want you to do is feel." He covered his head with my dress.

My fingers dug into the fabric of the sofa as Devin's hot tongue traced the seam of my swollen, aching pussy.

He pulled my thong to the side and repeated his slow torture. "You're so wet."

He continued his torment, making my body catch fire and scream for more.

"Devin, please."

"What do you want, baby?" He blew onto my aching core. "And be specific."

"Devin James Camden, if you don't fuck me with your mouth this second, I'm never going to have sex with you again."

"Now, we can't have that."

His lips captured my clit and without preamble, my body detonated.

I lowered one hand to grip his fabric-covered head and arched up to meet the rhythm of his tongue. My body prickled with goosebumps and my mind clouded with the cascade of emotions my orgasm brought forth.

"Damn, baby. You were ready for me. Let's see you do it again."

"No." I shook my head. "I need you to make love to..." I stopped my request as a knock sounded on the door and it opened.

"Dev, Sam, I think..." Ashur came to an abrupt stop. "Oh, for the love of God. I can never unsee this. Dammit, Devin. That's my sister."

CHAPTER TWENTY-ONE

Close to nine a.m. the next morning, I stared at myself in the mirror of the quaint bathroom in Dev's cabin.

Today was the day I'd enter a new phase of my life. Something I'd never dreamed of doing when I was a child. A pang of hurt hit my heart, reminding me of the fight with Papa the night before.

I had to accept I'd never be the daughter he wanted, and he'd never be the father I'd wished to have. At least I had the rest of my family: Mummy, Ashur, Veer, and all the Camdens.

What surprised me most was Richard's change of heart. He'd sat down with me and Jacinta to apologize for his behavior. He seemed genuinely affected by Papa's words and actions. He told us the whole evening had put a mirror in front of his face and shown him how he was heading down the same road as Papa. The last thing he wanted to do was isolate himself from his children. Then, he'd offered to assist me with the drafting of my statement for this morning. And this was before Devin and I'd told anyone about the pregnancy.

After learning he was going to be a grandfather, he'd smiled and said the kid was exactly like his father, since Devin was conceived during the beginning of Richard's first bid for Senate.

His effort to connect with me was a start to mending the hurt he'd caused, and I was going to take it. At least I had one father who wanted a relationship with me.

"Are you ready?" Jacinta peeked around the door of my bathroom.

"Almost. Let me put on some lipstick."

"That dress looks better on you than it ever did on me."

"I am a good three inches shorter than you. I'm just happy I can walk in it without tripping."

"Whatever, you know you look gorgeous. It's too short on me, but on you, it looks classy, polished, with a hint of high fashion and sexiness." Jacinta leaned against the doorframe and grinned. "Did you read the polls? I'm ahead."

"Yes, I did, Ms. Frontrunner."

According to the polls released twenty minutes ago, Jacinta was favored over Decker for her party's spot on the ballot. And Veer had a cult following of his own. As a war hero and a staunch supporter of veterans and the military, he had endeared himself to a segment of Texas politics who would rarely, if ever, vote for him. Now he had a twenty-point lead over the incumbent.

I was almost positive he was going to become the new Texas governor in four months.

As I set the makeup on the counter and turned to face my beautiful best friend, I noticed her wringing her hands together.

"What's wrong?"

"Nothing. No, really. I only wanted to say..." She paused and took a deep breath. "Thank you."

"For what? I'm the one who should be thanking you."

"For standing up to the Deckers and Sanderses of the world. I wish I had the courage to face the political fallout from revealing what happened to me. You make me think it's possible."

"It is," I assured her.

"No, Sam. My party is changing, but they aren't ready for what would happen if I came forward, and I'll never get any future presidential nomination as I'm poised to do now."

"I know, Jaci. No matter what, I will always have your back."

It would never be fair on anyone's part to judge her or others who'd suffered any form of violation—physically, mentally, or through reputation.

She came up to me, wrapping her arms around my shoulders and then pulling me in for a tight hug.

"I love you, Samina."

I squeezed her back. "I love you too."

Jacinta released her hold on me and dabbed at the corners of her eyes.

"Okay, enough sap. We have to go out there and face the mob. Excuse me, I meant the media."

Immediately, my stomach knotted and rolled, bringing the urge to throw up. The funny thing was that I wasn't sure if it was nerves or being pregnant.

"Thanks for bringing my mind back to reality."

"My pleasure. Want some fizzy water? You look like you're about to hurl."

"I'm good. Where's Dev?"

"I'm here," he shouted from the cabin's living room. "Ash and Veer have just arrived. They will be on the stage behind you with our parents. Tara also sent word Representative Jones filed your paperwork."

My hands shook as I tucked a strand of hair behind my ear.

The train had left the station.

"Okay, let's do this."

My candidacy wasn't just about me wanting control of my life anymore. I was doing it for women like Jacinta, who didn't have a choice in how they had to keep their secrets. For anyone who'd had someone in power take theirs away.

My phone beeped, telling me everything was ready for the press conference.

Dev stood as I walked out of our room. He cupped my face, kissing my forehead.

"Any anxiety?"

"A little, but I've got this."

"You'll be perfect. Just think of everyone in their underwear."

I scrunched up my nose. "That is a chilling thought."

We walked out of the house and toward the stage area and media pit. I wasn't sure how Jacinta had managed to transition from a holiday party to a patriotic campaign stage, but I was grateful.

I approached our families and nodded in their direction. They followed behind me as I took my place next to Veer. He was going to introduce me and then I'd be on.

"Ladies and gentlemen of the press, Samina Kumar will make a statement regarding her recent media coverage. Please note, she will not be accepting questions at this time but will be available at a later date."

Veer gestured for me to move behind the podium.

I stared into the crowd. The normally spacious and manicured flower- and tree-lined lawn at the entrance of Jacinta's estate was filled with cameras and reporters. There were police officers positioned along the fence and gates, blocking anyone who thought to trespass. And a giant American flag hung from the front balcony of Jacinta's house.

A tremor shook my body.

All of these people were here because of me. The moment I opened my mouth, I'd start a new chapter in my life. I would no longer be a celebrity attorney or the secret lover of a federal judge. I'd become a politician, ready to make a difference.

I could do this. I was going to do this.

Taking a deep breath, I began.

"Ladies and gentlemen. I'm sure, you've seen and heard about the pictures released to the public yesterday. Let me give you the context in which they were taken, so you may understand the kind of men who orchestrated the events of the last twenty-four hours and have been representing the great states of Washington and Texas.

"With any serious and committed relationship, one's experiences ebbs and flows. During one particularly tough day a few months ago, while I was in my home shower, Spencer Miller, a known tabloid reporter, broke into my house, took pictures of me, and threatened me. I was alone, emotionally distressed, sitting on the floor, and defenseless.

"Fortunately, my husband had security features installed in our bathroom, which allowed me to alert the authorities. Spencer Miller was arrested and charged with breaking and entering as well as voyeurism in the first degree.

"During a probe into the incident, investigators discovered Senator Grey Decker was responsible for hiring Spencer Miller and then selling the pictures to Senator Anthony Sanders. Subsequently, those images were offered to my former client, Clint Bassett, for release on his radio and Internet shows.

"You may ask why these two men would go after me. It's very simple. They fear for their positions in Congress.

Jacinta Camden and I are very popular in our states as well as very viable candidates against Senators Decker and Sanders. They thought to shame me and destroy my credibility as well as that of Ms. Camden. After all, I am married to her brother, and any scandal touching me will affect her bid against Senator Decker.

"Now to prove my accusations. At this moment, the Attorneys General of Texas and Washington, as well numerous other women and men in the political realm, are receiving thumb drives filled with evidence linking the senators to their conspiracy against me.

"It is time to stand up to those who abuse the privilege of working for the citizens of our country. It is time to change what is moral and acceptable behavior of those who preach one thing and behave in a different manner.

"Today, I stand before you as someone who is part of a new movement to remove all those who view their positions in Congress as a career and a right versus the privilege it is. I stand before you, not as a victim of immoral men, but as a fighter.

"I stand before you as a friend, a colleague, a wife, a sister, and the future senator of Washington State.

"I am Samina Kumar-Camden. Candidate for United States Senate."

A roar of applause erupted, as well as a barrage of questions, in spite of Veer's announcement. Jacinta and Veer came to each side of me and linked their fingers with mine.

"Smile pretty, kids," Jacinta whispered, so no one else

could hear. "This is a picture-perfect moment. A conservative, moderate, and almost-liberal onstage in support of each other."

"You had to throw that jab in there, didn't you?" Veer muttered.

Jacinta responded with an, "Of course, I did."

I mentally shook my head and smiled at the crowd.

"We can do this," I said with a sense of pride and excitement.

"Yes, we can." Veer squeezed my fingers and then lifted them in the air, with Jacinta following the same action. Another wave of cheers echoed out of the crowd.

After a few more minutes, we walked away from the podium and down the steps toward our waiting families. They cheered and clapped, including Richard, who kissed me on the cheek.

Tears prickled my eyes and my heart filled with happiness. I knew the road ahead was going to be tough, filled with nonstop challenges, but with these people in my corner, there was no doubt I'd succeed.

Devin came toward me, offering me his elbow. "Well done, Senatorial Candidate Samina Kumar-Camden."

He hadn't known about the name change. I'd kept it a secret. We were moving to make our marriage as solid as possible, and I thought it would be a sweet gesture to hyphenate my name.

"Thank you, Judge Camden," I said, slipping my arm into his.

"You were right," he said as we walked down the path onto the property.

I glanced to my side. "About?"

"There are enough Senator Camdens in politics. It's time for a Senator Kumar-Camden."

"I couldn't agree more."

"I do have one condition before we move forward."

I paused midstep and lifted a brow. "Of course, you do."

"I want to fuck celebrity attorney Samina Kumar one more time before she becomes Candidate Kumar-Camden."

"I believe that is definitely on the agenda."

The End

Read the next book in the Politics of Love Series

https://books2read.com/Senator

ABOUT THE AUTHOR

Inspired by her years working in corporate America, Sienna loves to serve up stories woven around confident and successful women who know what they want and how to get it, both in – and out – of the bedroom.

Her heroines are fresh, well-educated, and often find love and romance through atypical circumstances. Sienna treats her readers to enticing slices of hot romance infused with empowerment and indulgent satisfaction.

Sienna loves the life of travel and adventure. She plans to visit even the farthest corners of the world and delight in experiencing the variety of cultures along the way. When she isn't writing or traveling, Sienna is working on her "happily ever after" with her husband and children.

Sign up for her newsletter to be notified of releases, book sales, events and so much more.
www.SiennaSnow.com

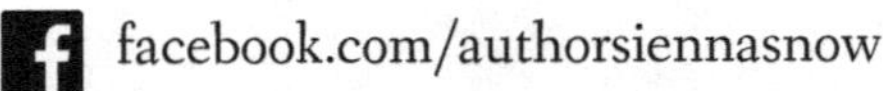 facebook.com/authorsiennasnow

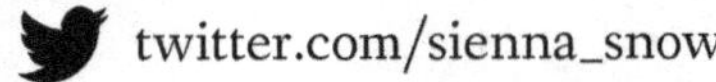 twitter.com/sienna_snow

instagram.com/bysiennasnow

goodreads.com/siennasnow

bookbub.com/authors/sienna-snow

Reckless Romeo (A Cocky Hero Club Novel)

Wicked Kings

Coming Fall 2020